ISBN: 978-1-7393935-5-7

CHAPTER ONE

C assandra sat downstairs in the living quarters watching her mother preparing the evening meal. She sensed that something terrible would happen that night to their home on the Cretan shore, but she struggled to imagine what form it would take. She thought it might have something to do with her mother's new boyfriend. She didn't like Lycos one bit. Besides, there wasn't room for him in their small, white mud-brick house. She'd got used to sleeping upstairs beside her mum in the bedroom in sight of the harbour, where she could dream of sailing to all those islands off the coast of Crete. But now she had to sleep in the room next door where Lycos had stashed all his fishing gear and she kept waking up to the smell of fish.

She didn't like the idea of sharing her mum with somebody else, especially a man like Lycos. She knew her mum, Callista, had been only fourteen years old when she bore her, which was young even by Cretan standards. And she still seemed more like an older sister than a mother. She was slim and beautiful, with soft brown eyes and long, dark hair – someone you could laugh and chat with long into the night.

But Lycos, the wolf, had spoilt all that. What kind of parents would give their son a name like that? He had only arrived a few nights ago, but she knew he was there to stay because he'd treated their house as if he owned the place. He looked about twice her mum's age and was loud and clumsy. He had a large, weathered face with oily black hair and cunning, greedy eyes and, the moment he walked in, his presence filled the room. He wasn't much taller than her mum but had broad shoulders and hips and large chunky legs. And he kept talking in a loud voice and making silly jokes that even her mum didn't laugh at.

Then she kept thinking about the volcano. She knew it was a long way off, and her mum said it was nothing to worry about, but it kept popping up in her dreams. She and her mum first heard about the problems on Thera when travellers started arriving from the island in their thousands. They didn't mention a volcano. All they talked about was earthquakes. The ground beneath their feet had sent houses crashing to the ground and made their island unsafe to live in, they said. It was only the later arrivals that mentioned the volcano. You couldn't see it at first because Thera lay a day's journey by boat from the Cretan shore. Then two days ago, you could see whisps of smoke stretching in a thin column towards the sky. Yesterday, it had got worse. You could see the base of the volcano throw up intermittent puffs of grey lava flecked with flames, creating a distant haze of ash and debris.

But Thera was a long way off. She was more worried about the problem on their doorstep. She looked lovingly at her mum bending over the fire, humming a tune to herself as she prepared the evening meal. She wondered again why they couldn't get along together, just the two of them. Her mum seemed to read her thoughts. 'Be nice to Lycos,' she pleaded, pushing back her hair as she turned to face her. 'He's only been here two days. He has a good heart. I'm sure you'll like him once you get to know him.'

'Greetings! Look what I've brought for our dinner!'

She winced as Lycos barged into the enclosed space, dangling a large seabream on a hook. He gave her mum a playful pat on the bottom as she stood over the fire and came and sat opposite Cassandra at the small wooden table. 'Have you had a good day?' he asked. 'Did you get up to any pranks? I remember some of the pranks I used to get up to when I was eight years old!'

'I'm ten.'

'Ten, eh?' he raised his eyebrows in mock apology and grinned. 'You look young for your age—just like your mum. I like children,' he added. He gave her a friendly leer and pronounced it 'chil-deren'. 'Have you seen the sky tonight?' he asked. 'It's amazing!'

'Am-a-zing!' Cassandra muttered as she got up and went to the door.

The moment she stepped outside, Cassandra wanted to scream for help—but the words stuck in her throat. She'd walked into a new and frightening world. She peered into a foggy mass of grey and—beyond that—a thick column of flames and smoke rising from that small, fixed point on the horizon.

This wasn't 'amazing'. She gasped for breath. Something terrible had happened. 'Mum! Mum!' she cried. 'Come and look outside! The sky's on fire!'

Her mum came and placed an arm over her shoulder. 'What's the matter, Cassandra? What are you looking at? Oh, in the name of Zeus! It's the volcano!' She pointed at the source of the flames. 'That's Thera!' she cried.

The base of the distant volcano had widened, and huge clouds of smoke rose skyward, releasing rocks and flaming ash, to rain down again in a thick curtain obscuring the view. Cassandra watched spell-bound, as the smoke and flames surged upwards—just as she'd pictured it in her dream. Then she lowered her gaze and stared at the fixed red mass of the volcano, imagining what would happen when that vast weight of molten rocks slid into the water.

'What's all the fuss about?' Lycos asked, wandering out to join them, with a glass of wine tilted towards his lips. 'Bad news for the people of Thera, but that island's miles from here.'

Then they all heard it—the distant rumble of an almighty, unending roar; the sound of half an island tumbling into the ocean. Even Lycos stopped smiling.

'That's the end of Thera,' said Cassandra's mum. 'I doubt if anybody left on that island will live to tell the tale.' Cassandra felt her mum's arms tighten round her shoulders as she pointed down the slope to the beach two hundred yards away. 'I've seen this once before,' she said. 'The water's receding now as if it's being sucked in by the volcano – but look out there! Can you see it?' Cassandra caught the fear in her mum's wide blue eyes, and it made her shiver.

'Well, you probably can't see it because of all the smoke and flames,' her mum said in a more matter-of-fact voice, 'but that last splash will cause the waters to rise—I don't know how high but twice the height of our house.' She clutched Cassandra's shoulder. 'You do understand, don't you, my dear?' she urged her. 'Any moment now, the waters will come towering towards us.' She pointed up the sandy slope behind the house and said, 'If we don't get onto higher ground—and I mean much higher ground—the wave will wash all over us.' She stared at the sea again and cried, 'Look! Can you see that thin white line of surf? That's the top of the wave. It's coming closer now! Help! It's thundering towards us!' She swung round and gave Cassandra a push. 'Quickly,' she urged her. 'You're still in bare feet. Get your sandals, and we'll make a run for it!'

That was the last thing Cassandra heard from her mother as she rushed into the house. She had just time to place the sandals on her feet and untether the goat and watch it race away up the slope. Then, just as she stood poised to make a dash for it, she felt a mighty arm block her chest and knew she was going nowhere.

She had a strange feeling about that arm. It began to open out into a thick, leathery wing. She wriggled in desperation to get away and screamed, 'Let me go! I need to reach my mother. Who are you anyway?'

The tall stranger released his hold and stared down at her. He had neatly curled brown hair and wore a pleated white robe like herself and, apart from the fact that he was twice her height and had wings instead of arms, he looked almost human.

'I have come to save you,' he said. She wanted desperately to believe him, but he didn't sound excited by the idea.

'Who are you? Are you an angel?' she asked.

'I'm a messenger. That's what angels are. The God, Poseidon, sent me.'

'But why? And what about my mother?' she asked.

'In a few minutes,' said the messenger, 'that wave will sweep over this land and destroy anyone or anything in its path. Your mother might be lucky. Who knows?'

'But you could save her!' she protested.

The messenger shrugged. 'I do what I'm told,' he said. 'Poseidon is angry with the inhabitants of Thera and Crete and has decided to punish them.'

She might as well have been talking to a block of wood. She turned and watched her mother racing up the slope, with Lycos not far behind her. At that moment, her mother turned and noticed her talking to the angel. That was the last she saw of her.

'I know my mother will be safe,' she said. 'She's a good runner. But you still haven't said why you are saving me!'

'Because you are Poseidon's granddaughter. Don't ask any more questions. I'm an angel, not a tour guide. Just climb onto my back and let me get on with my job!'

He bent down and Cassandra did as he instructed her, fastening her arms round his chest and her legs round his belly and clung on like mad as he raised his wings and soared high above the roof of their dwelling. Then, to her surprise, she discovered that she couldn't fall off even if she wanted to. It felt as if she'd been glued to the angel's skin, which seemed fine for the time being but might be painful when they came to separate.

Below her, she could see the huge wall of water surging over the shore, knocking down every obstacle in its path. In the distance she could see people running for their lives, struggling to reach higher ground. But then she squeezed her eyes tight shut, not wishing to see any more, just desperate to believe that her mother was still alive.

CHAPTER TWO

C assandra clasped the angel's chest as they soared up into the night sky. She stared down at the harbour of Amnisos. The houses on the waterfront had gone. She spotted a few stray timbers and wrecked sailing vessels tossing on the rising waters. She craned her neck to see what had happened to her house, further inland, but that too must have vanished beneath the tidal wave. She could still see tiny figures racing to reach higher ground. She prayed that her mother would be among them. She took comfort from remembering how her mother had looked back and seen her talking to the angel. Without that, she felt sure she'd have turned round and tried to rescue her.

Thoughts flashed through her mind as she rose higher and higher, safely glued to the angel's back. If Poseidon had been prepared to rescue his granddaughter, why couldn't he rescue her mother too? She figured that must be because her mother was a mere mortal, which meant that the man she had married was Poseidon's son. She wondered who he could have been. He had to be famous, which would make her a bit famous as well.

And he had to be at least half-immortal—which would make herself a little bit immortal too – she wondered which bit. Her mother never spoke about her father, so perhaps he was one of those immortals who was famous for doing something bad. If her mother was famous, it would always be for doing something good. She made another silent prayer to Poseidon to rescue her from the waves. Surely her mother had more right to be saved than anyone she knew. The moment she touched ground, she'd get back to Amnisos and find her. Her mother was an athlete. She felt sure she'd have made it to higher ground—unless she'd felt obliged to wait for Lycos. That would be typical of her—always putting others first! Cassandra didn't feel sure that she'd have done the same herself.

They seemed to be travelling at huge speed. Those wide wings bore her higher and higher in an almost vertical ascent. The air felt cooler now as they travelled northeast, away from the volcano. As soon as she realised that she had no way of falling off the angel's back, she began to relax and let her thoughts wander. Her mind roved backwards and forwards from the home she had left to her unknown destination until she gave up the struggle to think and just closed her heavy eyelids and nodded off.

She had no idea how long she had slept, but the moment she opened her eyes she noticed that the angel had already begun his slow descent. She peered down at the still, blue waters of the Aegean with its scattering of islands. Memories flashed through her mind of when she was six years old, and she'd made the long sea journey with her mother in a small Athenian fishing vessel to her future home in Amnisos. Athens had seemed like a village at that time compared with the wonders of Minoan Crete. She wondered if Athens was still like that. They spoke Greek there, she remembered—a bit different from the language of the Cretans, but she often spoke Greek with her mother, so she reckoned she knew enough to get by.

Then the thought of her mother made her feel terribly alone. 'Where are we going?' she asked the angel.

'Athens,' he said.

She'd guessed that.

'That's where your father, Theseus, used to be king.'

'But he was married to—'

'He was married to many women. Your mother was one of them.'

So that's why her mother never talked about her father, she thought. He was a famous warrior and free to do as he wished. 'Is he still famous in Athens?' she asked.

'He is famous throughout the Greek world. He killed the minotaur, remember?'

So, her father was famous for killing things—though Cretans said that no such creature existed in the first place, so he was probably a liar too. She wasn't sure his fame would help her since he wasn't famous for helping her mother. And he'd never come to visit her either. She was sorry he was dead before she could tell him what she thought of him.

Still, her dad was the son of Poseidon, which made him at least half-immortal. Perhaps that would buy her a few favours when the angel left her alone in the world to fend for herself. What could she do—climb trees and collect olives in baskets? She'd seen kids her age doing that. Or maybe she could milk goats or herd sheep? She'd done that before. She could wash clothes in the river, then beat them and hang them out to dry. She hated that kind of work, but she'd do it, if pushed. Best of all would be if she could work on a boat bound for Crete—a small fishing boat maybe, because the larger boats required a strong team of male rowers.

She gripped the angel's sides as he completed his descent. She could see the village of Athens sparkling in the clear blue air with its small square houses scattered like cubes of salt round the slopes of the Acropolis. And she could see a row of similar dwellings stretching some of the way towards Phaleron where the boats lay moored, just as her mum had described it to her. She knew her mum had been one of the young maidens at the palace, educated to become brides to the Mycenaean warriors that ruled the city, but Theseus must have stepped in and chosen her for himself. Half-immortals were allowed to do that, she supposed. It was like getting your first share of the pudding.

At the very top of the hill, she spotted a crude temple—nothing like the grand temples of Amnisos—surrounded by an area of rough grass. In the front of the temple stood the marble statue of a goddess. She had to be Athene, she supposed. She was meant to be very wise. She remembered her mother saying that the Athenians thought they were the cleverest people in the world, so that's why they named their city after the goddess of wisdom.

They landed with a bump in front of the temple. 'Poseidon told me to give you this,' said the angel, towering above her now. He handed her a linen bag which jingled with small pieces of silver. 'They won't last you long to barter with,' he warned. 'I suggest you start looking for work. I believe domestic slavery is quite popular in these parts.'

'I don't like you either,' she thought, but instead she said 'Thank you for the journey,' and watched him head off into the sky.

She suddenly felt scared and alone, but she hadn't time to think of that because quite a crowd had gathered round the temple and watched the angel's ascent. She had the feeling this might play in her favour, because it would make her seem important in their eyes. She saw a market in progress to the right of the temple. Fishermen, farmers, potters, and weavers stood behind trestle tables calling out the price of their wares. She found it hard to make out what they were saying. The language seemed similar, but different from the language they spoke in Amnisos. She'd get used to it, she supposed.

Most of the buyers broke away from the tables and hurried towards her. She soon felt hemmed in by a hundred inquisitive faces. 'Who are you?' they wanted to know. 'Are you a goddess? Where are you from? Was that Hermes we saw descending from the sky?' She could hear them murmuring amongst themselves:

'She must be a nymph—a dryad perhaps. Look at her chiton! It's embroidered too. You won't find many folks in these parts that can afford an expensive garment like that! She must be Cretan. Well, they can afford that stuff in Crete! Look at the jewels stitched into the lining! She must be a princess at least!'

She felt the crowd closing around her, eyeing her up and down and poking her to see if she was real. One old lady, grey-haired, bent and frail, and clothed in black linen, reached out a gnarled hand and fondled her hair. 'Ain't she lovely!' she cried. 'You can tell she's someone special.' Cassandra felt the other hand reach for her shoulder and noticed a sudden lightening of her burden as the lady disappeared into the throng. The linen bag which the angel had given her had gone!

Then, at the back of the crowd, she saw a young boy who looked not much older than herself, stop the lady in her tracks, whip the bag away—despite her protests—and run towards the temple. In full view of the crowd, he brushed back his mop of curly brown hair, held the bag aloft and went and sat on the temple steps, giving Cassandra a friendly wave, and beckoning her to come and join him. She felt a warm glow of relief at finding an ally in these hostile surroundings. She smiled at the crowd and made her excuses for slipping away. After a bit of a struggle, she managed to break through and make a run for it, and soon she was sitting beside him on the temple steps.

'I'm Alexis,' he said, smiling as he handed over the bag. 'I saw you descending from the sky. It wasn't the brightest idea of that angel to dump you here among these thieves and scoundrels.'

'My name's Cassandra,' she said. 'I don't think that angel liked me much,' she admitted.

'Well, Cassandra, welcome to Athens!' he said, giving her hand a firm shake. 'You've already got a fair idea of what it's like in this rathole, but we're not all cheats and swindlers. How old are you, by the way?'

'I'm ten.'

'Well, I'm twelve. But judging by the way you landed in this place, you seem to know what you're doing. Would you like to tell me about it?'

Cassandra smiled. She didn't know where to begin. She wanted so much to have someone she could talk to. Her mind was still back there on the shores of Amnisos, with friends of her age, who liked to play together on the beach or stroll into town and chat and look at the goods on display in the market stalls. And now, quite out of the blue, she'd been snatched from the wave and dumped in this strange place, not knowing if her mother was still alive. And she was famous! Her father was Theseus, the former king of Athens! Her grandfather was Poseidon! It was all so new and exciting! But a little voice told her she'd walked into a trap. The angel had placed her here because that's where the people in charge wanted her to stay. And all she wanted to do was get back to Amnisos.

Then she remembered that this boy with the kind twinkle in his eyes had asked her a question. He was not only a head taller but seemed many years more grown-up than herself. She hesitated. 'I'd love to tell you everything,' she said, 'but first I'd like to spend some of this silver buying us both something to eat. I'm starving.'

Alexis placed a restraining hand on hers. 'Then be my guest. I'm sure the laws of hospitality are the same in your country as they are in mine.'

She followed him in silence down the slope, glad to find a friend in this alien place. 'It's lucky that angel didn't deposit you on the other side of the hill,' he said over his shoulder. 'That's where King Cecrops has built his palace.'

'Why? Is he dangerous?' she asked, hurrying after him.

'No, he's just a bloodthirsty tyrant, like all our Mycenaean leaders. If one of his guards had spotted you in that chiton, with those jewels sewn onto the lining, he'd soon have hauled you before the king as a suitable marriage prospect.'

So that was the trap! She shivered at the thought. She knew her mother had been through all that, but her mother had parents living in Athens at the time. 'I told you! I'm only ten years old!' she protested.

'No matter! He'd have you trained for the role of becoming a warrior's wife, or even a queen—you'd spend your days learning the art of sewing and weaving—and all the other stuff that these wives are supposed to know. The food would be good, though,' he added, turning to face her with a cheeky smile. 'I guess you'd like that bit.'

They'd reached the bottom of the slope now and she felt content to follow him in the darkening gloom down one of the narrow, cobbled streets leading off from the base of the

Acropolis. 'Mind your step!' he warned, 'and keep an eye on those windows too. People chuck all their waste into this street. I mean all of it!'

'Where are we going?' she asked.

'I'm taking you to my house,' he said. 'It's not far. My father's a potter and I'm his apprentice.' He squeezed her hand and added, 'though I plan to have my own business in the future.'

CHAPTER THREE

Alexis' house looked like her own house in Amnisos, two storeys of baked and whitewashed mudbrick, resting on two solid layers of white stone. The interior looked similar too—except that her own house lay tossing beneath the waves on a distant shore. Wooden steps on her right led to the bedrooms upstairs. One point she'd noticed in its favour as she'd followed Alexis inside was that, since it was the last house in the street, there was an open space beyond where his father could sit and work at his potter's wheel. The wheel would be brought inside at night, she realised. It was far too precious to be left to the mercy of thieves.

She followed Alexis into the house, which was dimly lit by four tallow candles placed at the corners of the living space. She stood behind him and smiled and nodded as he told his parents in an excited voice who she was and how he'd met her at the market. His mother, Hestia, was a stout woman with broad shoulders and a round smiling face and black hair gathered in a plait which reached to her shoulders. She opened her arms wide and gave Cassandra a hug. His father, Daedalus, looked a bit like an older version of his son. He had grey, grizzled hair and a creased, weathered face but with the same mischievous twinkle in his eyes as he said, 'Welcome to our house! I must say it's a pleasure to meet such a pretty, young lady from Crete—especially one that's just dropped out of the sky! Miracles like that don't happen every day in Athens, I can tell you—leastwise not in our part of the town.'

Cassandra blushed and stared at the floor, but Daedalus just laughed and said, 'Don't worry. You've come to the right house, Cassandra! There are bad folks in this town who will try to take advantage of your fame and fortune—but you'll be safe with us, I assure you.'

'That's enough of that, dad' Alexis said. 'The poor girl's starving! She hasn't eaten since she left Amnisos!'

An enormous smile spread across his mum's face. She bustled round, laying an extra space at the rectangular table and searching among the shelves for extra food to add to the meal.

'Ah, Crete!' Daedalus sighed, taking the seat by the wall and beckoning Cassandra to sit opposite him at the table. 'No country that I know of makes pottery the way they make it in Crete. It's so natural, so lifelike—the sign of a civilised society, I'd say. I love Cretan ware—their wall paintings too. All those dancing girls and birds and flowers—the sign of a society at peace.'

'I'm afraid my dad's gone off on one,' said Alexis, sitting beside her, 'but I know what he means. We only produce the plain colours and simple patterns. But that's what most people seem to want, providing it comes in the right shape to satisfy their basic needs—vases, bowls, dishes—and amphora for wine.'

'Alexis is a good potter like his dad,' said his mother, handing out steaming bowls of soup and chunks of bread fresh from the oven.

The soup was fragrant with onions, carrots and celery and all sorts of ingredients that Cassandra couldn't put a name to. She dipped her bread in it and thought it was the most delicious meal she'd ever tasted. And after that came small silvery fish served with olives and herbs, and then freshly baked almond cakes, washed down with retsina—a resinous yellow wine. Cassandra had never drunk wine before, so she took their advice and diluted it with water, but it still left her feeling a bit dizzy.

With her new friend by her side, she began to forget her worries. She shut her eyes for a moment and let her thoughts run away with her. She needed to get back to Crete, but maybe Alexis would come with her. Maybe his parents would come too! They could hire a fishing boat and perhaps make the journey in careful steps, stopping off at islands along the way. That would be safer than throwing themselves entirely at the mercy of the wide-open sea. And then she could walk the streets of Amnisos and ask around until she managed to get reunited with her mother...

She looked up and realised she'd been dreaming. That angel had tricked her! All that talk about finding a job – that had just been a cruel joke. He had placed her before the temple for all the world to see. That made her a walking prisoner. Sooner or later, they'd come for her and lead her to the Palace, just as they'd done with her mother. And then they'd put her to school where she'd be trained until she was old enough and judged fit to become a warrior's wife. How many times had her mother told her about all that! She didn't want that life! She wanted to stay here with this delightful family.

She thanked Alexis' mother for the delicious meal—'the best meal I have tasted in my life,' she said. Then she turned to Alexis' father and said, 'The Cretans may be the best potters, but surely the Mycenaeans are good at some things too. They make wonderful objects, don't they, from gold, silver, and bronze?'

Alexis' father gave a grim nod. 'Yes,' he said, 'I suppose you could say they are good at anything to do with death. They make wonderful helmets and spears and plates of armour and then—when their warriors die in battle—they shove all the wonderful treasures they have created into their graves.' He laughed and added, 'However, you can live a good life here in Athens, providing you keep a low profile and stick to a humble occupation that's needed, like farming or fishing or making pots. Then you're unlikely to be drafted into the army.'

Cassandra thought of the crowd on the Acropolis watching her land on the back of an angel. How did that fit in with keeping a low profile? She tried to stifle a yawn, but Hestia noticed and led her up to the bedroom next to her own. She grabbed the mattress, which used to be Alexis' and placed a fresh one down for her. She then gathered fresh sheets and a pillow, and tossed them onto the mattress, wishing her a peaceful night as she carried Alexis' bedding downstairs.

She needed to be alone for a bit, she thought, as her head hit the pillow. There was so much to think about. That angel had treated her like a rag doll. He hadn't asked if she wanted to be rescued from the wave. She could have run up that slope like her mother and ended up safe in Amnisos. Well, probably! Instead, he'd landed her in Athens, which was a dangerous place. Her mother had told her what it was like once you got stuck in the marriage pool. But she'd been lucky—so lucky!—meeting this family. Even her friends' families in Amnisos hadn't shown her such warmth and kindness. And Alexis—he was so thoughtful and kind. She'd never met a boy like that before. It showed her that not all boys were as bad as she'd imagined. And this mattress the mother had given her was so comfortable. The pillow too! It was so hard to think in such a comfortable bed...

CHAPTER FOUR

It was early morning when she woke up. She must have gone to bed early, she thought. She heard no sound from the parents' room next door, so she got dressed and tiptoed downstairs, careful not to wake Alexis who lay flat out on his mattress. She often did this in Amnisos, she thought, as she slipped out of the door, so why not here in Athens? She used to go down to the beach before breakfast, while her mother lay sleeping, to enjoy the wonderful feeling of owning her surroundings at a time when nobody else was awake. She wouldn't stay out long. She didn't want to upset this family who had been so good to her. She would just explore the broad wasteland beyond the house—and maybe pick a few mushrooms if she could find any—to offer them as a present.

The wasteland didn't look too promising. It was just a vast, dusty plain ending in a long line of stunted trees, just visible when she screwed up her eyes. But the birdsong brought the place alive. The starlings were going at it like mad, clustering in a swarm above an olive tree, then changing their minds in a frenzy of twitters and shooting off in a different direction. She spotted two blackbirds guarding their nest and a cluster of thieving crows roaming the land like bandits. Then, to her delight, she looked up and spotted a pair of eagles circling the sky high above her head.

She passed a few olive trees scattered over the parched soil, but hardly enough grass for mushrooms to flourish there. Then, in the distance, she thought she saw a stream. It was certainly greener in that area, so there must be water around. She hurried off in that direction and, sure enough, saw a small patch of grass on either side of a stream where she found mushrooms growing in small clumps. She stuffed as many as she could hold in the folds of her chiton and set off for the house.

She hadn't realised until that point how far she had walked or how long she had been away. The parents must be up by now. Would they be angry with her? She'd never stayed overnight in other people's homes before. She went as fast as she could without spilling her load and—with a sudden sense of guilt and shame, broke into a run and arrived, panting, at the door of the house.

Hestia came to the door. 'Come in, dear!' she said in a soft voice. Her dark hair hung loose, and her face looked drawn and downcast. Cassandra got the feeling that she'd been crying.

'I've brought you some mushrooms.'

'That's very kind of you, dear,' she said in a husky voice. 'I'll put them in this bowl.'

'Where are the others?'

'They've gone with the guards from the Palace. Come and sit down, dear, and I'll tell you about it.'

They sat together at the table and Hestia explained how two guards had knocked on the door and demanded to see 'the girl.' When they learned that Cassandra was missing, one of them—Hestia thought his name was Janus—said 'We'll take the boy instead. You can have him back when you bring us the girl. Alexis resisted, so they started to knock him about. They had weapons. We couldn't stop them!'

Hestia started to cry. 'My husband has followed them to the Palace to protest. Much good will that do him! Before he went, they broke his potter's wheel, so he won't be able to practise his trade anymore. I don't know what we're going to do after this.'

Cassandra burst into tears. 'It's all my fault!' she sobbed. 'If I hadn't gone out, they'd have taken me instead and you wouldn't have had all this trouble.' She realised that the game was up. It felt like having a rope tied round her neck and being taken to prison. 'I'll go with you now,' she said, 'and do what they want, so long as Alexis is safe to go home.'

Hestia stood up and threw her arms around her. 'It's not your fault, my little chicken!' she said. 'It's just the way things are in this place. My husband will be back soon, so you'd better wait for him. We'll have to plan our next step.'

Cassandra knew what lay in store for her. She was the grand-daughter of Poseidon, so they'd release Alexis once they'd got her safely stuck in the marriage pool. She gritted her teeth. If it ever got that far, she hoped she'd be allotted a husband who died in battle. That would offer some light at the end of the tunnel.

But what about Alexis and his family? They wouldn't be able to live in Athens much longer—not after those guards had broken his potter's wheel. He could buy another one, but she guessed they'd break that too. He was a marked man now. They aimed to put him out of business.

The door opened and Daedalus walked in. 'You've heard the news then?' he asked as he sat down heavily at the table. He ran his hands through his grey hair and said, 'I don't know what we'll do next. There's no arguing with these people. Once they've marked you down as a threat, that's the end of it.'

'How's Alexis?' asked Hestia, handing him a glass of milk.

'He's a good lad—well, you know that! He doesn't complain, though they knocked him about something dreadful.'

Cassandra stood up. She wanted to burst into tears again, but she felt too angry for that. 'I'm going to enter the marriage pool,' she said. 'That's the deal, isn't it? And then they'll release Alexis.'

She could see the relief on his face. He stood up and said, 'I'm coming with you.'

Cassandra hesitated. She thought of those kids she'd met in Amnisos. Once they knew they could hurt you, they'd just want to hurt you some more. Bullies were like that. They already had

Daedalus in their sights—he had nothing left to bargain with, so there was no way they'd honour their deal to release his son. 'Come with me as far as the Acropolis,' she said. 'Let me do the rest on my own. I'm just a girl offering them the swap they want. The moment they see you, they'll just try to mess you around.'

'She's right, you know,' said Hestia, placing an arm over her shoulder.

Daedalus nodded. 'Well, let's get it over with,' he said.

'I shall miss you all so much,' Cassandra said as they walked up the street together. 'I have never met a real family like yours before. Do you think we will ever see each other again?'

'Let's hope so,' said Daedalus. 'To tell the truth, I have it in mind to leave this place and set up our business elsewhere.'

'Will I be able to find you—if I manage to escape from the Palace?'

'I'll leave a message for you. You can be sure of that.'

They had reached the foot of the Acropolis and she stopped and gave him a hug. 'This is where I leave you,' she said. 'Alexis will be with you shortly. Please give my love to Hestia.' She grinned and wagged a finger at him. 'You haven't seen the last of me! You can be sure of that!'

'I think those palace guards may have taken on more than they can handle!' he said with a sad smile as he waved goodbye.

CHAPTER FIVE

She'd play it by ear, she decided, as she arrived at the massive arched entrance carved out of huge blocks of granite. The important thing was to sound polite and willing – otherwise she'd arouse suspicions, and she'd never be able to escape. The metal gates already stood open, so she walked up the steps to the doors of the palace where two armed guards stood at attention.

'I've come for the boy you've arrested,' she said. She judged from the grins they exchanged that they were the ones who'd arrested him.

'Tell her, Janus,' said the tall one, with the scar and the floppy hair. 'We had a bit of fun with him, eh!'

'You had, Dracon,' said Janus, the shorter man, who looked the more dangerous of the two and seemed to be in charge. He turned to Cassandra and said, 'He's down below, feeling a little bit poorly.'

'Then bring him up, I want to see him. That's the deal, isn't it? He's free to go and now you've got me.'

'I'll bring him up, but I can't release him,' said Dracon, walking down the steps to the business part of the palace, where she guessed that they kept their stores and prison cells.

When he left, Janus shuffled his feet and said, 'Hang on! I'll need to seek advice about this.' He disappeared into the palace, locking the door behind him.

Dracon reappeared holding Alexis by the scruff of the neck. He looked in a bad way. He could hardly walk, and she spotted black and yellow bruise marks on his cheeks. 'What have you done to him?' she asked. 'You could have killed him! Let go of him!' she cried.

'If I let him go, he'll fall to the ground,' said Dracon...' See!'

'Let the curse of Poseidon be upon you!' she screamed, running to place her arms around him and help him to his feet. 'Can you manage to get home on your own?' she whispered in his ear. 'It's me they want—not you, but it's going to be easier to settle this business without you here for them to bargain with.'

'Are you sure? I can't leave you here on your own!'

She checked that Dracon wasn't listening and added 'Yes, sure. If you stay here, they'll use you as hostage to stop me escaping. I'll be back shortly. I'll think of a way. Don't you worry!'

'But—!'

'No buts! This is the best way, believe me!'

She held him tightly to her chest, then watched him stumble away down the steps. She ignored Dracon, who protested weakly, 'Here! You can't do that!' Then she heard him ask in a humbler voice. 'Is it true that you're Poseidon's granddaughter?'

'You'd better believe it!' she said, determined to give no quarter. If he was stupid enough to think that made a difference, she might as well put the fear of the god into him.

At that moment, Janus returned to announce, 'The King wishes to see you. He seems willing to offer an exchange.'

'That's already been done,' said Cassandra with an innocent smile. 'Just as you promised,' she reminded him.

As she followed the guards through the door that led to the palace, Cassandra knew that she didn't stand much chance of getting out of that place any time soon. Her best hope lay in pretending to like it there.

The first chamber she passed was the armoury; there were openings along the top of the wall so that you could see the spears and helmets and suits of armour hanging on display. The door to the next room lay open. Even before she reached it, she knew this would be the room where she'd be forced to spend most of her days. She could see the women now, seated at separate tables attending to their looms. She didn't see any girls of her age in that room. She spotted a few that might be as young as thirteen or fourteen, the rest a bit older. A spiteful grey-haired lady in a black robe stood by the door wielding a thick, knobbly cane. 'Hold out your hand, Irene!' she said to one of the older girls who stood before her with a pale face and tears forming in her soft blue eyes. 'You are here to work, not to chatter. Now repeat what I have just said.'

'I am here to work, not to chatter,' said the girl, staring at her instructor with meek, pleading eyes.

Thwack!

'Now the other hand! And repeat what I told you!'

'I am here to work—'

'That will do—and stop howling!'

Thwack!

'Discipline. That's what I like to see!' said Dracon in passing.

'No, you don't!' she thought. 'What you like to see is cruelty and bullying. She had seen and heard enough.' She hurried after the guards, who had already reached the end of the corridor and turned the corner, past the banqueting hall to the audience chamber. They stood there whispering to each other.

'You're on your own now,' said Dracon. 'All you've got to do is knock on this door and, when you hear a voice cry 'enter!' you must walk in and prostrate yourself before the King. 'Prostrating' means falling on your knees and bending down so that your head touches the ground. And once you've done your prostrating, you remain on your knees but raise your body from the ground and state your name, your parentage, and the nature of your request. Oh, and by the way, don't mention that your father was Theseus. He's no longer popular in these parts.'

'How do I know which is the king?'

'He's the big man sitting at the centre of the audience table. 'I've done my bit now, so I'm off—so go ahead, knock!'

'Thanks. I'll tell my grandfather how helpful you've been.'

She noticed a wave of relief on his face as he nodded and hurried off. 'Got you!' she thought as she knocked on the door.

She waited a few seconds, then heard a deep gravelly voice call, 'Enter!'

Trembling in every limb, she pulled the massive door open and, without looking at the men gathered behind the table, made for the centre of the room, and prostrated herself on the marble floor.

'Arise and state your name and the nature of your request!' boomed the gravelly voice.

Perched on her knees, which was difficult - adjusting her chiton on a marble floor—she gazed up at the blurred images of the men staring down at her from the other side of the thick, oak table. There seemed to be seven of them, and the one in the middle—a big, ugly brute who resembled a bear, with a broken nose and shaggy brown hair running down to his beard—had to be Cecrops, the king.

'My name is Cassandra, granddaughter of Poseidon,' she said in a clear voice, 'who rescued me from the tidal wave that struck my home in Crete. I am grateful for the opportunity you've given me to start my education at the Palace, but I am only ten years old, and before that I humbly request a month's leave to return to my home in Crete.'

She felt her knees knocking together as she stood and waited for an answer. Seconds passed in silence before it came.

'Well, you can't!' roared the gravelly voice.

Cassandra guessed this would be the answer, but she thought it was worth the try. 'I am afraid I may not understand the lessons,' she said, 'and this may hold the other girls up.'

'There is only one lesson you need to learn,' growled Cecrops. 'That's to do what you're told. Go! You have said enough! If you say any more, I might be angry. When that happens, people tend to get hurt. You can wait outside until we have decided your fate.'

CHAPTER SIX

S he stood outside the door and shifted from one foot to another. She had to get a message to Alexis, who'd proved to be the best friend she'd ever had, besides her mother—a boy who'd rescued her from the crowd in the marketplace and then been cruelly beaten by those guards just for giving her food and shelter. She thought of those girls in the tapestry room. She guessed she'd be joining them soon. Surely, they'd know of a way of conveying messages!

Just then the door opened and one of the notables seated at the table came out to greet her and lead her into the room—a junior official with a thoughtful expression who grabbed a chair from the stack in the corner of the audience chamber and placed it in the centre of the room for her to sit on. 'I think that you will be more comfortable like that,' he whispered, resuming his place at the end of the table.

'We have come to our decision,' said Cecrops, bending his head towards her and softening his speech in a grotesque effort to sound kind and fatherly. 'We feel that it is only right that you, a child of aristocratic stock, but having no aristocratic parents on hand to guide you, should stay in our care, learning all the domestic and social skills that belong to womanhood.' He paused and moistened his lips. 'You are somewhat younger than most of our girls,' he added, 'but I have no doubt you will learn fast. And you will be fed and provided with dormitory accommodation. And then you can look forward to the time when one of our noble warriors considers you a fit young lady to become his bride.'

'Thank-you very much,' said Cassandra, staring at 'the noble warriors' gathered behind the table and tightening her jaw muscles to hide her fear and loathing.

The young man came over, took Cassandra's chair, replaced it in the stack, and escorted her out of the room. 'I guess that wasn't the decision you wanted,' he said, 'but I will try to make it as comfortable for you as possible. The younger girls are having lunch now, so I will take you to them and no doubt they can tell you more than I could about their daily programme.' He opened a door before the entrance to the Weaving Room and led her down some stone steps to a grassy square enclosed by the four granite walls of the palace. There she found four girls, a few years older than herself, squatting round a low table in their brightly embroidered chitons. 'My name's Georgios, by the way,' he said. 'I guess I'll leave you to it.'

The girls jumped to their feet and gathered round her, making welcoming noises and admiring her hair and the jewels in her chiton. Like her, they all had glossy, black hair—either stained or natural—folded and pinned in a way to show off their pretty faces. They'd all heard about the angel, which made them somewhat in awe of her, touching her skin to see if it was real. The tallest one among them, Alethea with the mischievous smile, pulled her towards the table where they sat and picked at their light banquet of bread, anchovies, olives, lettuce, and grapes.

A large, jolly girl with a broad, smiling face called Thalia, sitting on her other side, whispered in her ear, 'You're sitting next to 'The Truth,' right?'

Cassandra recognised that Alethea's name meant 'truth', so she wondered what was coming next.

Thalia pointed at Alethea and said, 'It's funny they should give that name to such an accomplished liar!' The other girls laughed, and Alethea joined in the laughter.

Then Chloe, a tall, timid girl with an anxious expression, looked up from the table and asked, 'What do you think of Georgios?'

Thalia laughed and said, 'What's not to like? Strong arms, muscular chest, and he's polite too. He doesn't throw his weight around like some of these warriors!'

'My parents say I can marry him in a year's time when I reach the age of fifteen,' said Chloe. 'It's very convenient because his family owns the farm next to ours. Georgios is a common name for farmers, you know.'

'If he's a farmer, I'd say you're in luck,' said Arete, the thoughtful girl seated on Chloe's other side. 'He won't be called off to fight in these wretched wars.' She turned to Cassandra and added, 'Otherwise, he's no different from the rest of them. He just hides it better. It's power and status that matter most to him.'

At that moment, a bell sounded, and Alethea turned and explained to Cassandra, 'Our next class is Spinning and Weaving. And after that comes Singing and Dancing—the dancing can be fun. Just sit at the back and go to sleep like me and the teacher won't bother you much.'

Cassandra felt pleased to be welcomed among such friendly company, but a little disturbed too. Perhaps it was because they were only a few years older than her, and already thinking about marriage. They didn't seem to have much choice about the life they chose to lead or even the man they married. It felt like being among a flock of lambs trained up for the slaughter.

Then she thought of Alexis and the life he led with his family. That was the life for her! She'd stick around with these girls—they seemed nice enough—but she'd have to find a way to escape.

CHAPTER SEVEN

After her first day, Cassandra found life tough at the palace—almost unbearable. Cretan palaces had no walls, as the people were mostly farmers and tradesmen. They weren't like these Mycenaeans. They didn't need thick granite walls to defend themselves from warriors like themselves, obsessed with pillage and plunder. The people here had never tasted freedom. At least she felt glad that she wasn't a slave. There were hundreds of these flitting around the palace—most of them women—clothed in shabby, torn chitons and trained to perform the most menial tasks while hovering like shadows in the background. Even the women of a higher class had none of the freedom she'd enjoyed in Crete. They were fed and pampered until they were judged old enough to be selected as brides—often to seasoned warriors twice their age. She supposed that's what had happened to her mother until Theseus had come along and jumped the queue. She wondered how her mother must have felt about that, as a girl of fourteen, dumped in a strange country by a man she hardly knew, with a baby on her hands and the gift of a few jewels and ornamental trinkets to see her through for the rest of her days.

The girls she'd met so far spent half their time gossiping and devising ways of ending up with the man of their choice. But Cassandra hadn't reached that stage yet. She didn't want to reach it! Besides, she was young and Cretan! She was Poseidon's granddaughter!—which had already proved a useful card to play if you played it on the people dumb enough to believe it meant anything.

She'd got up that morning, prepared to face the worst moment of the day—knowing she had to face four hours of weaving and spinning in the dreaded Weaving Room. But even that moment had its compensations because of Irene, the girl she'd seen savagely beaten by the teacher the day before. Irene was, by general consent, the sweetest and prettiest girl in the room. She was seventeen years old and already betrothed to a warrior twice her age. She didn't speak about him much, but then she was too meek and submissive to complain. Irene was one of the best weavers in the group and, as soon as Cassandra entered the room, she took her hand and led her to the bench beside her. 'Don't worry! It's easy, once you get the hang of it,' she whispered. 'I'll show you what to do.'

All the girls knew that the teacher—the old witch who issued instructions from her desk—picked on Irene out of spite just because she was pretty. But Cassandra resolved that this day was going to be different, so when the moment came, and the teacher waved her thick knobbly stick and called Irene to the front of the class, she pressed Irene to her seat—despite her whispered protests—and walked up instead.

The teacher stared at her in horror. 'What are you doing? You're new here, I believe. I asked for Irene.'

Cassandra stared at the teacher with contempt. 'Irene was teaching me to follow your instructions,' she said. 'So, if anybody should be punished for speaking, it should be me, as I was the cause.'

'Very well then,' said the lady, raising her eyebrows and waving her stick.

'On the other hand, I wouldn't want to upset my grandfather, but it's your decision.'

'Your grandfather?'

'Have you noticed that the sky's getting darker?'

Well, the threat worked once on a superstitious old lady, but it wouldn't work with most people, she thought, as she returned to her seat. Still, it was fun while it lasted!

The other classes passed without mishap. She liked the dancing class best when a Cretan musician stepped in with his lyre and made them all stand in a circle around him and perform elaborate movements, weaving in and out to tunes she remembered from her childhood trips to the market square in Amnisos.

The girls she shared her lunch with greeted her with cheers. 'At least you put that old witch in her place!' chortled Alethea.

'That Irene is such a dope. She has no idea how to stick up for herself!'

'As you do,' observed Arete tartly, reaching for another grape.

'Yes, Alethea knows how to get what she wants,' agreed Thalia, gulping down an oily pilchard, letting the juice dribble down her chin. 'It's my belief that even some of the men are scared of her.' Thalia had a hearty approach to eating, as she had to most things. She nudged Alethea in the side. 'The men here think they hold all the cards, but we know how to shuffle the pack, don't we?' she added, giving her a wink. 'How's your Georgios' by the way?' she asked Chloe. 'Is he still Gorgeous?'

'He's a good man,' said Chloe quietly.

'Hey, where are you going?' asked Thalia, seeing Cassandra rise from her seat.

'I've just thought of something,' said Cassandra vaguely. She walked off up the steps to the dormitory and lay on her mattress for a while to collect her thoughts. She had just remembered that this day was her birthday. She was eleven years old this day! That made a significant milestone in her life, and she wanted to celebrate it. Well, she'd do that by making herself a promise. She'd find some way of getting out of this place soon and, once she'd done that, there'd be no stopping her! She'd find Alexis and her family and together they'd travel to Crete where she'd meet up with her mother. With that sorted—in her own mind, at least—she walked back down the stairs, ready to face whatever the afternoon held in store.

CHAPTER EIGHT

Despite her latest resolve, two days passed and still no news from outside those walls. Cassandra tossed and turned on her mattress in the dormitory that night, struggling to decide her next move. What made it more difficult was that she liked the girls in her group—especially Irene and the four younger ones - and some of the activities weren't too bad either. She would like things even more if it wasn't just a fancy prison.

And what about Alexis? In the condition she had seen him last, she wondered if he was even in a fit state to walk the streets—and if he did, would he get arrested? And what about his parents? They'd seen what the guards could do to their son. You never knew with this regime. Once they had marked you down as a threat, the best way to survive was to keep out of sight. So, it was up to her to make the first move. All she could think about was how to get out of this place and meet up with Alexis and his family again. She had to do it soon, because—the way

Daedalus had been talking—he might be getting ready to sell his house and go abroad. What if he'd already done so? He'd promised to leave a message, but what if he couldn't?

She guessed that he'd wait for her. Would the whole family be prepared to make the journey to Crete? It was a big ask but, remembering what Daedalus had said about Cretan pottery, the idea of heading for Amnisos might appeal to him. But the moment she managed to escape the guards would come knocking at his door. She'd have to get there first. It didn't take long to get to his house. But what if the family had already gone? She'd just have to get to the harbour and beg or barter a place on a boat heading south across the Aegean. And then she'd be free to search for her mother—praying that she was still alive. She'd no idea how she would do that.

The mattress she'd been allotted lay close to the wall, and the girl who slept next to her was Alethea. 'Having problems, little one?' Alethea whispered—they all called her 'little one'—'Can I help you in any way?'

'I need to get out of here. I need to see my boyfriend called Alexis.'

'A boyfriend?' asked Alethea, giggling, and inching closer so that her mischievous dark eyes came inches from her face. 'A bit young for that, aren't you?'

'Well, not exactly a boyfriend, but a real friend. He helped me when I first arrived, and he introduced me to his family. They're good people.'

'And what does he do?'

'I don't know exactly,' she lied. Alexis was her friend—he didn't belong to anyone else.

'Hm. There is a plan I can think of, but once you're out, you won't be able to come back—not without a good whipping. Are you happy with that?'

'I don't want to come back. I want to return to Crete.'

Alethea giggled again. 'Well. You're mad, but I admire your pluck,' she said. She lay on her back and gave the matter some thought. 'There's only one time the gates open, and that's at six o'clock in the morning when the wagon brings in the supplies,' she decided. She rolled over and clutched Cassandra's hand. 'You know—the food and drink!' she said. 'I'll go with you to distract their attention and you can slip away, unnoticed.'

'Won't that get you into trouble?'

'No, the driver fancies me! When I wake up early, I often go to the gate and stand chatting with him,' she added. 'That way, he gives me milk or grapes—whatever I fancy. He leaves his goods at the base of the Acropolis and carries the crates up the steps by hand, so there's plenty of chatting goes on.'

'So tomorrow morning?'

'Don't worry! I'll wake you up on time.'

Cassandra lay there flat on her back, going over the plan in her mind. She couldn't see a catch to it. Slip out of the gate while Alethea stood talking with the tradesman. Then race down the hill while the man delivered his wares. She soon heard Alethea snoring. She was a cool customer, dreaming up a scheme like that, then dropping off to sleep.

Her thoughts were interrupted by the sight of Arete, standing in her white nightgown by the door to the dormitory with a finger to her lips and beckoning her to join her. She followed Arete through the door, and they stood outside at the top of the steps. 'I heard Alethea's plan,' Arete whispered. 'Don't listen to her. She means to turn you in, I know it.'

Suddenly, it all made sense. Of the four girls in their little group, Alethea was the one she least trusted. She remembered what Thalia had said about her the first time they met—something about having a name that meant truth but being an accomplished liar. 'Why would she do that?' she asked.

'Ask Chloe,' she said, staring at her with her serious, honest eyes. 'We're all trapped in this marriage game. We don't get to choose the man we want. He chooses us—though our parents have a say, naturally. Alethea wants Georgios—the one that's betrothed to Chloe.'

'But would Georgios...?'

'Probably not. But any information that she feeds him—like your attempt to escape—that's valuable knowledge that will increase his power and influence. She's fed him other titbits before, but catching you red-handed, defying the rules of our society—that will make him a power to be reckoned with.'

Cassandra felt her eyes brim with tears of frustration. It was such a good plan, she thought—the only escape plan she could think of that might work. 'What can I do?' she asked.

For an answer, Arete fixed her steady gaze upon her and handed her a small glass vial. 'Alethea is a heavy sleeper,' she said.

'Sprinkle this powder on her face—all of it—and she will sleep for the next twelve hours.'

'And then?'

'Proceed with her plan. It was a good one. But I won't be helping you, I'm afraid, beyond promising to wake you in a few hours, so that you can get some sleep before you set off.'

Cassandra gave Arete a grateful hug and followed her back into the dormitory, where she emptied the contents of the vial over Alethea's upturned face and lay on her mattress, where she fell into a dreamless sleep.

She awoke with a start in the semi-darkness to find Arete sitting on her bed, stroking her hair, and coaxing her into wakefulness. 'You have time,' Arete whispered. 'The tradesman won't have arrived yet at the base of the Acropolis. Your best bet is to hide on the right of the archway, where he makes his entrance. The archway projects a foot or so from the wall so that when he opens that heavy door, he's unlikely to see you.'

By the time Arete had finished speaking, Cassandra had dressed and collected her few belongings, which she placed in her sack slung over shoulder. She threw her arms round Arete, and held her tightly, planting a kiss on her cheeks and whispering her thanks for saving her from a certain disaster. Then she slipped through the door and ran down the steps to the long corridor, turning right past the Audience Hall and right again past the Weaving Room until she arrived at the open door at the top of the steps where she had made her first entrance. She stood in the half-light, seeing the deserted courtyard, then ran down the steps and hid there, figuring it safest to remain out of sight until she heard the tradesman's approach, when she would take Arete's advice and hide by the doorway.

Waiting was the worst bit. It seemed like an hour before she heard the heavy tramp of the tradesman's steps as he carried his first crate up the hill. She made a dash for the wall on the right of the gate and stood there, flattening herself as best she could in the corner where the archway extended from the wall. Then clang! The heavy gate swung open, and the tradesman passed a few feet from where she stood, struggling with his heavy load. In a moment, she slipped through the gate and raced down the steps.

'Hoy!'

She froze in her tracks. Just before the gate closed, the tradesman had looked back and seen her. She was still on the path to the palace, she realised. She trembled and swerved to the left, where she'd be hidden from view and could mingle with strangers on the public path descending from the Acropolis. She couldn't hear any sounds of pursuit yet. The tradesman was probably informing the guards, she thought. And they would know where to find her! But she was safe for the moment, so she set off at a trot, slowing her pace whenever she saw a stranger heading in her direction. She raced down the steps towards the narrow lane that led to Alexis' house. She'd better warn the family of the impending danger and then hide out somewhere in that wasteland.

Brimming with nervous excitement, she knocked at the door. No answer—so she knocked again, a bit harder. She peered through the window and saw no sign of movement. Perhaps they were still asleep. She stood back and stared at the upstairs windows. No sign of movement there. What if they'd gone away? She had just begun to lose hope when an elderly lady appeared from the house next door. 'Are you Cassandra?' she asked in a kindly voice. 'Come in and I'll tell you where you can find them.'

CHAPTER NINE

C assandra did as the old lady instructed and sat at the small, round table in the far corner of the room. She trembled with the double relief of knowing that the guards would be searching the wrong house and that this kind lady knew where the family could be found.

The lady bustled around placing bread and milk on the table and grapes and honey which she scooped from a large earthenware jar. 'You must be hungry, my dear,' she said. 'Put a bit of that honey on your bread. My husband used to be a beekeeper, bless him, before he passed away. Now what is it I had to tell you? I made a list, so I wouldn't forget anything important. My name's Agatha, by the way.'

Cassandra saw the telltale lines of concern around the old lady's eyes. She knew that 'Agatha' meant good and thought it was the right name for such a kind old lady.

Agatha searched inside her woollen vestment and placed some jumbled objects on the table. This was her 'list' which made more sense to her than they did to Cassandra. 'That one's Daedalus,' Agatha murmured, pointing to a piece of pottery 'and that's a boat...' She fingered each object in turn and mumbled to herself as she recalled the message. Then she looked up and said, 'The family knew you'd find a way to escape, but they couldn't stay and wait where they were—not after what happened to their son.'

She reached over and patted Cassandra on the hand. 'He's recovered now, bless him!' she said. 'He wanted to go and get you out of that place, but his parents said it would only make things worse. Once they've marked you down as a nuisance, these people, you're best off keeping out of sight.'

'So where are they now?' Cassandra asked, feeling her pulse race with expectation.

'Well now, they've sold their house and bought a boat. It's waiting in the harbour at Phaleron. And they'll wait for you there two weeks, they said, and if you don't come within that time, they'll leave a message where you can find them.' She looked up and smiled at Cassandra. 'Well, you don't need that last bit of news, do you, dear?' she said, 'because you're a quick one, you are!'

Cassandra felt a sharp pang of guilt. She thought of that poor family forced to sell their house—all because of her! But she couldn't suppress her joy at hearing the news. That meant they'd decided to accompany her to Crete—or at least part of the way on her journey. 'Is it far to Phaleron?' she asked.

'It's a bit of a way, if you're travelling on foot—a good walker like you could make it in about an hour. There are quicker ways of getting there, but then you're liable to attract attention, which is the last thing we want, dear, isn't it?'

Cassandra heard a loud knock at the door and shivered, thinking it might be those guards from the castle come to take her away, but the old lady leaned forward and patted her hand. 'Don't worry, dear,' she said. 'That will be Brontës. He's called that because of his size. He comes round every day to check on me and see if you're here yet. He'll escort you to the harbour. You'll be safe with Brontës, I assure you.'

The old lady shuffled to the door and gave a nod of satisfaction when she opened it and found the giant standing in the doorway. Her hunched frame barely reached the belt round his waist, and he had to bend down so that his brown, shaggy hair touched her head as he shook her frail hand. He had a club and a dagger clipped to his belt. 'Is this the girl?' asked Brontës in a deep throaty voice. 'Charmed to meet you, I'm sure.' His blue eyes lit up and his mouth opened wide in a smile. He bent down and extended his huge hand, and Cassandra just managed to enclose three of his fingers in a handshake. 'Well, the earlier we set off, the better,' he said in his deep voice, after a moment's reflection. 'There will be fewer people on the road at this hour.' Cassandra thanked the old lady for her help, and followed him out of the house, excitement surging through her veins at the thought of seeing the family again—at the harbour too, which was one step nearer home.

'The guards at the palace probably know where we're heading,' she warned Brontes. 'Once they've checked the house, they'll ask around and head for the harbour.'

'Thanks for the warning,' said Brontes. 'We can both keep an eye out, young lady, and I'll deal with that problem when it arises.'

Cassandra pictured how he'd deal with the two guards. He didn't seem overly bothered by the prospect, she thought, so neither should she.

Brontes forged ahead in giant strides, and she had to skip to keep up with him. The town, with its narrow streets, soon gave way to farmland, and the road ended in a wide sandy path. On either side she saw fields of parched vegetation sprinkled with olive trees, or meadows where goats nibbled what grass they could find, and pigs rooted for acorns under the scrawny holm oaks. Judging from the size of the buildings, these were small farms where the owners eked a living, feeding their families and earning a little bit extra by selling their produce at local markets. Still, Cassandra's heart filled with joy, just to be out in the open air, seeing wildflowers on either side of the path and hearing the familiar mew of buzzards circling overhead. It reminded her of her home in Crete, and she felt a sudden yearning to be on a boat with Alexis and his family heading for Amnisos, where she could ask around and achieve her dream of being reunited with her mother.

'We're nearly there,' said Brontës. She noticed more people on the path now, all heading from the harbour. These people were mariners or fishermen who greeted Brontës as they passed or edged round him with respect.

It was all going so well, Cassandra thought, when suddenly, out of nowhere, she spotted the two guards from the palace, heading up the path behind them, armed for business in breast-plates and helmets. Brontës came to an abrupt halt and turned to face them, placing a hand on his dagger.

'Ah! Just the young lady we're looking for!' cried Dracon in a taunting voice. 'We guessed you'd be heading here. Your presence at the castle has been sorely missed.'

A crowd of onlookers gathered at the side of the path as the two guards approached. Cassandra clutched Brontës' arm at the sight of their unsheathed swords. 'Get behind me, Little One,' Brontës urged in a hoarse whisper. 'I need my hands free to deal with these scoundrels.' He planted his huge legs in the centre of the path, with the club in his left hand and the dagger in his right. 'This young lady is in my care,' he called out in his deep voice. 'If you want her, you'll have to fight me for her, and you will surely die!'

Cassandra kept her eyes fixed on Janus. He was the dangerous one. She saw how he stood back, planning his approach. It was Dracon who made the first move. He rushed forward, aiming to drive his sword into Brontës' stomach, but Brontës simply stepped aside and swung his club, striking him a huge blow on the head which knocked him to the ground unconscious. He then finished him off with his dagger, urged on by the shouts and cheers of the crowd. But just then, Janus saw his opportunity. As Brontës stooped over the corpse, he ran towards him and pierced the side of his chest with the edge of his sword. Had not Brontës made a sudden swerve, the sword would have gone through his heart. As it was, it just made him mad. He gave a roar of pain, and plunged his dagger through Janus's neck, pinning him lifeless to the soil.

After a shocked pause, the bystanders rushed forward to help. There was no question whose side they were on. Two women ran to place salves on Brontës' wound and bind it with clean linen, while a group of local farmers carried the corpses away for secret burial, far from the prying eyes of the palace. Then came the question of what to do with Brontës himself. To everyone's relief, he was well enough to answer. Since he was no longer safe in these parts, he explained, through gasps of pain, his dearest wish was to be borne to the harbour, along with his young charge, and to join her on her voyage,

And so it was decided. Six farmers searched the surrounding area for enough wood and rope to provide a makeshift stretcher and, with Cassandra walking alongside making feeble attempts to cheer him, they bore him the short distance to the harbour's edge.

By this stage, the news of the young daughter of Poseidon and her giant travelling companion had spread among the crews of all the fishing boats and sailing ships in the harbour, and it was not long before Cassandra saw Alexis in the distance running towards her with his parents following along behind. He looked wonderfully recovered from his injuries. He gave her a long hug and congratulated her on her escape from the Palace. 'The news travels fast here,' he said. Then he glanced at the giant on the stretcher and added, 'That man must have saved your life. Once he recovers from his wounds, he'll be a great person to have around on our journey.'

Alexis' parents were not far behind. Daedalus thanked the stretcher bearers and asked them to perform the last but most difficult task of carrying their heavy burden down the stone steps of the harbour to the point where the boats were moored, keeping the stretcher level as they did so. They lowered their burden at the foot of the steps and seemed eager to be off and away. Cassandra noticed a steady stream of mariners gathering their belongings and heading in the opposite direction.

'As soon as the Palace gets wind of what happened to those guards, Daedalus explained, they'll be swarming all over the place.' He turned to Hestia, who was busy placing a new dressing on Brontës' wound. 'How's Brontës?' he asked.

Hestia had taken Brontës to her heart. She sat beside him on the rough ground, placing ointment on his wound with infinite care. 'He's in great pain,' she said in a soft voice, 'but thankfully the wound's not deep. He'll be better in a week or two.'.

'Good. I'll bring the boat a bit closer, and we'll find a way of getting him on board.'

'Where are we going?' asked Cassandra.

'I think Aegina's our best bet,' said Daedalus. It's quite a large island, and it's only an hour or so away. Besides, they don't like the Palace in Aegina, so we should be safe there for a few days, while Brontës recovers from his wounds.' He pointed to a large sailing vessel not far from the harbour's edge. 'That's our ship,' he said, 'the one with the high prow and the square red sail. It's a Cretan vessel—smaller than the Cretan ships of war, equipped on either side with fifteen banks of oars—but it's bigger than the normal fishing vessel. I've had to adapt it to our use, selling off some of the oars to make room for our passengers and provisions and—look!—my new potter's wheel! He turned and asked Cassandra with a smile, 'So what do you think?'

'I think it's brilliant!'

She was glad to hear about the potter's wheel. She remembered what Daedalus had said about Cretan pottery and guessed that meant he saw a future for his family in Amnisos.

Alexis had already climbed down onto the boat moored closest to the harbour's edge. 'Are you ready?' he called, stretching out a hand for Cassandra to join him. She seized his hand and jumped, laughing as she landed in his arms, nearly pushing him into the water. Daedalus took a more cautious approach, lowering himself onto the first boat with his back to the harbour and groping for something solid to cling on to as he made his way to join them. 'I'm naming this vessel 'The Cassandra,' he announced with pride, standing amidships with his hand on the mast. 'The only problem is that there's no room to lie down, so these vessels are not built for long voyages. We'll have to travel in short bursts—'island-hopping' they call it. Then he frowned as he stared across the water, where Brontës lay on his stretcher. 'We'll have to place him in the bow,' he decided, 'with a pile of cushions behind his back, but there's no room for him to lie out flat, poor fellow!'

CHAPTER TEN

It was a short voyage to Aegina, though an agonising one for poor Brontës as the jolting of the waves stretched and strained his back, causing the wound on his side to bleed again. Alexis' mum sat by his side, dabbing the cut, and offering him sips of powdered willow bark dipped in honey, which eased the pain a little. But Brontës was the first to join in the cheers when they saw the northwest shore of Aegina with its sandy beaches loom out of the mist. And, above and beyond it, they could see the temple of Apollo presiding over the sprawling town of Colona, the capital.

Many of the mariners and fishermen in the harbour—a mixture of Mycenaeans and Cretans—gathered round to greet the new arrivals. They all wanted to know about Brontës—they couldn't stop talking about his size. They thought he must be a god or a legendary hero, but when they saw his wound, and learned he'd got it while killing two guards from the Athenian palace, their admiration and sympathy had no bounds. Some of them rushed off to collect a stretcher and soft bedding, others to fetch blankets and food and even a canopy. They were back in a while—a laughing, chattering mob—lifting Brontës onto his cushioned stretcher and, beckoning Alexis' dad to follow, leading them away from the harbour to a nearby sandy beach, where they placed the stretcher on the sand, with the canopy over it to protect his head from the midday sun. The canopy, secured by stakes at the four corners, proved wide enough for Cassandra and her adopted family to place their baggage, bedding materials, and their few possessions behind Brontës on his stretcher.

Some of the crowd lingered by the canopy, sharing their lunch with the new arrivals and chatting about the sea life and the places they had visited. Cassandra suddenly felt a moment of sadness and shame as she realised that she had been in Alexis' company for a whole day now without once having tried to speak to him alone. This was the boy who'd been badly injured, just for trying to help her, and she'd not even had the chance to thank him. She saw him standing alone, a little apart from the group, scanning the horizon. She ran up and tapped him on the shoulder. 'What are you thinking about?' she asked.

He turned to her and smiled. She loved the way he looked at that moment—always so kind and thoughtful. 'I'm thinking about our voyage,' he said, 'and all the exciting places we'll visit—including Crete, of course. That's our destination, isn't it? We've got to find your mother. That's our goal, isn't it?' He stopped and gave her a quizzical look. 'And you? What are you thinking?'

She felt herself blushing and her words came out in a rush. 'I'm thinking of you,' she said, 'and how kind you've been, and how you rescued me from that woman on the first day and how you introduced me to your family, and then got badly injured by those guards and I haven't even thanked you.'

He patted her on the back. 'Well, now you have,' he said, 'but I admire your courage, so I'd have done it anyway.' He glanced at the group gathered around the canopy. 'I tell you what!' he said. 'The moment we arrived here, it's felt like being on holiday. Why don't we climb up that hill and explore a bit? I heard them saying there's a market up there beside the temple.'

She opened her eyes wide and gave an enthusiastic nod.

'I'll take that as a 'yes' then. I'll just go and tell my parents where we're going.'

A moment later, they set off on the winding path that led through scrubby grassland up the hill. As they approached the temple, the path became a narrow lane bordered by small terraced two-storey houses very similar to Alexis' home in Athens. The lane ended in a market square beside the chapel, like the one Cassandra had seen on the Acropolis. But the wares on offer looked altogether more rich and plentiful. The fish stall stood laden with octopi, squid, scallops, and anchovies, as well as sardines and seabream and larger fish she couldn't put a name to. And next door stood a lady doing brisk business selling apricots and figs and melons and pistachio nuts. But Cassandra had already eaten, and at that moment, her eyes lit on the pottery stall. She tapped Alexis on the shoulder and cried, 'Look Alexis!

Your dad would be interested in this—you too! All these pots are from Crete!'

'Maybe because I'm Cretan,' said the tradesman, a big man with a generous smile. He turned to Alexis and said, 'Forgive me for overhearing your conversation, but is your dad, by any chance, a potter? In that case, I would be most interested in meeting him. I'm always glad to exchange notes on the tricks of the trade.'

Alexis promised that his dad would return on the following day. Meanwhile, Cassandra's interest had been distracted by the items of jewellery on the next table—she couldn't help giving little squeaks of delight as she pored over the objects on display. There were gold beads, pendants, and ornate earrings, adorned with all sorts of jewels—lapis lazuli, quartz, cornelian, and green jasper. There was also a chest pendant depicting a Cretan god—she couldn't remember his name—flanked by two geese in a field, and the tiny gold earrings were in the shape of double-headed snakes encircling two pairs of racing greyhounds.

'I see these objects appeal to you,' said a kindly voice. She looked up and saw the grey-haired goldsmith observing her with amusement.

'That's because I'm from Crete,' she said.

'I guessed as much. What part of Crete, may I ask?'

'Amnisos.'

He gave a gasp of astonishment and stared at her as if he had just seen a marvel. 'Were you that girl who...?'

She nodded.

'People have been talking about it ever since—the people who survived the wave, I mean. I was lucky myself because my house lies on higher ground, but many buildings were destroyed, and their owners buried beneath the rubble. But you—you must be Poseidon's granddaughter. You've already become a legend in my hometown.'

'I'm going back there,' she confided. 'I'm looking for my mother.'

He nodded. 'Ah yes, I remember her now I come to think of it. She was a frequent visitor at my workshop. I even met your dad once, though he wasn't around for long. But your mother-—she lived in that little house along the coast...'

'Do you think she...?'

He screwed up his eyes, as if trying to visualise the scene. 'She was last seen racing up that steep slope, with that friend of hers stumbling along behind her. The people I know guessed that she probably made it, because the wave didn't reach so far inland.' He stopped and stared into the middle distance. 'You know what I'd do?' he asked. 'I'd consult the oracle. The main one is at Delphi, but there's reckoned to be quite a good one on the island of Delos. I'd ask there if I were you.'

Cassandra felt Alexis' hand on her shoulder and said goodbye to the goldsmith, thanking him for his advice and promising to visit him at his workshop the moment she arrived in Amnisos.

'I heard most of that,' Alexis told her. 'So, Delos is our next step on the journey, though it may be more than a day's sail. It depends on the wind.'

They set off down the winding path, feeling the evening sun still warm on their backs—in Cassandra's view, the best part of the day. The only thing she regretted was forgetting to bring her sack with all those valuable silver pieces that the angel had given her, and she'd never thought to use. She resolved to go back there the next day.

The first thing she noticed as they stepped down onto the beach was the large crowd still gathered round the canopy where Brontës lay in state. At a safe distance from the canopy, she saw that some of the fisherman stood tending a fire with a bronze grill placed over it, which filled the air with the rich fishy smell of the day's catch. They had more fish ready in buckets, adding them to the grill as soon the first fish were cooked. She screwed up her eyes, because of the smoke, and slipped under the canopy where Alexis' mum sat tending to Brontës.

Brontës lay in state, staring up at the roof of the canopy and beaming as Hestia applied soothing ointments to the wound on his side. 'I feel like a new man!' he said with a hoarse laugh, 'as the cannibals say in Phrygia. My wound is almost healed.'

'Well, almost,' agreed Alexis' mum, gripping Cassandra's arm. 'Stay here!' she whispered. 'I have a gift for you.' She foraged behind the stretcher and returned with a folding leather case. 'You came here with hardly any clothes,' she said, 'and you'll need them—especially when the winter comes.' She held the first item of clothing up against Cassandra's figure, confirming that it was right for size. 'One linen chiton,' she said. 'You can wear that tonight, and I'll take the other one away to wash. Then there's another chiton of the same size, but this one's woollen. You'll need this for the winter.' A smile of satisfaction appeared on her broad face at the sight of a job well done. Then she delved into the case again and held up a himation, or overgarment; the first one in linen and the second one in wool. After that, she handed Cassandra a bunch of silver brooches, saying 'you'll need these to fix the clothes on your figure in the way that suits you best.'

Cassandra gave a cry of joy and threw her arms round Alexis' mum, saying. 'I don't know how to thank you for this wonderful gift!'

'No thanks are needed. Your joy is my reward.' She replaced all the items in the case and said, 'Put it by your bedside for now, so that you can use what you need in the morning.'

CHAPTER ELEVEN

At sunrise the next morning, Brontës got up and strolled down the beach to the water's edge. He stood for a while, admiring the reflected light of the sun glistening on the tranquil surface of the waves. Then, he stumped back to the canopy and declared. 'Look at the sea! I can think of no better time than this to make our voyage to Delos!'

Alexis' parents looked at each other and shook their heads. 'Give it another day,' cautioned Hestia. 'I know you've made a marvellous recovery, but any sudden movement could stretch that wound wide open, and then you'd be back where you started.'

'Besides, we're not going to Delos. We're going to Kea,' said Daedalus.

Brontës' mouth hung open. 'Not going to Delos? I'd set my heart on Delos! I wanted to go to the temple of Apollo there and beg forgiveness from the God for those two men I murdered.' He stared at the ground in despair.

Cassandra emerged from the canopy and reached up and hugged him above the waist. 'You saved my life, Brontës,' she insisted. 'If you hadn't killed them, they would certainly have killed you, and then dragged me back to the Palace to be whipped and bullied until I did what I was told.'

Brontës studied their faces and gave a thoughtful nod, then added, 'but I'd still like to go to Delos!'

'We will, Brontës, we will,' Alexis' dad assured him, 'but the local fishermen have assured me that, in a boat such as ours, Delos is too far to reach in one day. Our best plan is to sail to Kea—we can do that this afternoon, and you can sit at the stern and relax. Then tomorrow it's all hands to the oars and we can reach Delos in one day's sail.'

Brontës' broad face relaxed at this news. Just then, he looked up and saw a local fisherman, laden with gear, who waved and hurried over to join him. The man shoved a spare fishing rod in Brontës' hand, and the two of them went off to spend the rest of the morning casting their lines from the water's edge. Cassandra was glad to see that Brontës only cast with his left arm.

Alexis and his parents were eager to speak with the potter. Like many Mycenaeans, they were attracted by the idea of restarting their business in Crete, and keen to learn how to create all those flowing lines, involving animals and birds and flowers and people going about their daily lives. Cassandra wanted to visit the goldsmith's stalls, but this time she remembered to bring her sack as she followed them up the hill.

Alexis and his parents headed for the potter's stall. Few people were around at this time of day, so Hermes the potter had time to greet them and show them the tools of his trade. Cassandra heard Alexis' dad explain that he couldn't buy any items at this time because no pottery would survive the voyage on their little boat. But they would soon be heading for Crete! And they hoped to visit him at his workshop! As the conversation became more animated, Cassandra slipped away to the gold-smith's table and bought the items she had most admired from the day before—two chest pendants for Alexis and his dad, and gold earrings for his mum. She noted with relief, as she placed the items in her sack, that she'd only spent half her silver pieces.

Just then, she heard the mingled roars and laughter of a drunken crowd rushing up the slope behind her. All hell broke loose among the market stalls beside the temple, as a swaggering crowd of young men—some of them fully armed—burst onto the scene, waving their weapons and shouting. They barged into the stalls, swinging their swords, grabbing any object that took their fancy and overturning the tables. Cassandra felt a tremor of fear when she recognised their Athenian accents. They re-minded her of the guards that Brontës had killed. She looked round and spotted Alexis, who grabbed her hand and rushed her to the back of the stalls where his parents stood among a throng of stall holders, nervously looking on.

At that moment, Cassandra saw to her relief that help was on its way. An angry crowd of fishermen and mariners came pouring into the marketplace from the path below, armed with knives and anchor hooks. Then, to her right, she saw townsmen approaching in a solid throng, dressed in full armour.

The young men were too hot-headed or drunk to know when they were beaten, so many of them ended up dead. Then came a moment of uneasy silence when the few rioters that remained threw down their weapons and realised that they were trapped. At that point, the townsmen stepped in and surrounded them, sorting the thirty or so captives into three groups and leading each group, strung like clothes on a washing line, to an uncertain fate in the town gaol. A group of townsmen stayed behind to help the stall holders recover the objects missing from their stall.

Cassandra turned her back on the spectacle and cried. She knew what had happened on the beach below without needing to be told. A huge wave of sadness shook her body, and she felt seized by an unstoppable flow of tears. Poor Brontës! He had been so kind, and brave and undemanding! Without him, she'd never have reached this island alive. She knew what he'd have done on that beach. He'd have foreseen the danger to their safety, as he always did, and doubtless left many corpses strewn on that beach. She thought of all those fishermen and mariners who had been so kind to them. She knew that many of them too would have died, coming to Brontës' aid.

And then she remembered those guards—who thankfully were dead now, and another dark thought entered her mind. You were never safe with these people. The Palace was like that octopus painted on Cretan vases. Once you offended these people, you were never truly safe. The Palace would extend its long tentacles and track you down.

She felt Alexis' arm on her shoulder—her best friend in all the world. 'Come on,' he said, reaching in the folds of his chiton for a scrap of linen, and using it to gently wipe her eyes. 'We'd better join this lot,' he said, pointing to the crowd descending the slope. 'Think of it this way,' he said. 'He was a good man, and he died a good death—he lived a life that any person could be proud of.'

She tried to think of it that way, but it didn't help much. She was just glad of Alexis' arm slung over her shoulder. As they approached the end of the path down the slope, they could hear from the cries of the crowd in front that the carnage had been at least as bad as they imagined. Many of the people around them had left friends on that beach and their descent became a stampede as the crowd behind them pushed forward, anxious to get to the beach to know if their loved ones were still alive.

As they stepped down onto the sand, everyone went silent. The crowd thinned out and became just lone individuals wandering across the vast space, searching among the strewn bodies for people they might know. Some had already found them and knelt huddled in grief around the corpses of friends or relatives. Other corpses—no doubt the corpses of the rioters—received no sympathy. Cassandra saw a small army of townsmen piling these corpses onto carts and dragging the carts across the sand to the grassy area on their right where the beach ended. There they dumped the corpses in a vast trench they had prepared for them and covered them up with earth. This operation virtually halved the number of casualties and enabled the crowd to search with more assurance for the bodies of missing friends. And some of those friends were thankfully alive, moving among them and able to explain the tragedy that had taken place.

Cassandra and Alexis saw a crowd gathered at the end of the beach and headed in that direction, knowing all too well what they expected to find.

'That's him. That's the noble Brontës,' said a fisherman, pointing to the huge body lying stretched out on the sand with blood pouring from two sword thrusts in his stomach. 'And that's the friend he was fishing with. If you'd arrived a moment earlier, you'd have found ten more bodies—and those would be the bodies of those rioters they killed.'

A short distance away, Cassandra saw a group of farmers and fishermen piling large blocks of granite onto the sand and forming them into a square, on which they placed a thick pile of dead branches and twigs. All over the beach, she saw other families erecting similar piles for their relatives. Then she saw Alexis and his parents emerge from the canopy, carrying Brontës' stretcher. She noticed that the fisherman's relatives had done the same for his friend. Several hands were needed to raise the two stretchers onto the pile. Then the onlookers tossed incense onto the wood and set the funeral pyre alight. They stood round it, making all the traditional prayers for fallen warriors, then each recalling the individual acts of kindness and bravery of their friend until long into the night. When it came to Cassandra's turn, she said, 'He was our rock—so humble and kind through and through, but brave as a lion.' Then she burst into tears. But at the same time, she felt a comfort in knowing that his goodness had not gone unrecognised.

CHAPTER TWELVE

The next morning, Daedalus received a visit from the local demarch, the official responsible for local affairs. Cassandra could see them talking at the foot of the slope behind her as she sat on a cushion outside the canopy, breakfasting on a bunch of grapes washed down with a glass of milk. She guessed that the subject of their conversation might be serious because of the way they waved their arms about. And they went on talking for a long time, but adults did that, she noticed. It just worried her the way that the demarch kept turning and pointing in her direction.

'What was all that about?' she asked Daedalus, when he walked back across the sand to join her.

'Oh nothing,' he said vaguely. 'It was about the oracle.'

Cassandra had an uncomfortable feeling in her stomach. She thought of that angel rescuing her from the wave and landing her in Athens in full view of the crowd in the market. That was supernatural. That's what oracles were about!

'In that case,' she said, 'it must have something to do with me!'

'You're right, Cassandra,' he said, sitting beside her. 'Those Athenian prisoners they took yesterday, when asked why they rioted, said that the granddaughter of Poseidon must return to Athens and her protectors must be destroyed.'

'Did the oracle say that?'

'Yes, the one at Delphi.'

'Then why didn't they grab me?'

'They would have done, but they were too drunk and disorganised to manage it. Besides, they killed Brontës who was there to protect you and that was a good half of what they came for.'

Cassandra shuddered. 'And do you think I should return to Athens?' she asked.

Daedalus smiled and patted her on the shoulder. 'By no means!' he said. 'Oracles can't be trusted. The one at Delphi is the worst of the lot. It used to be controlled by Thebes. Now it's Athens. Cecrops has bribed the priestess and tells her what to say.'

'So why does he want me to return to Athens?'

'Propaganda! You're Poseidon's granddaughter, remember! When you're old enough, he wants to marry you off to one of his warriors—preferably himself. You'd like that, wouldn't you?

'It's not funny!'

Daedalus gave her shoulder a good squeeze. 'Of course, it's not funny,' he said. 'It means that we need to get to Crete that little bit faster, because any island in these parts has links to Athens.'

Cassandra felt safe in his hands and began to relax. She looked down at the workforce that had just arrived on the beach. 'Aren't those the prisoners? She asked.

'The men in uniform are the guards. The ones that are half-naked are prisoners—they've been sent to clear the remains of the funeral pyres.'

'And after that, will they go back to prison?'

'No, after that they will be executed. It's a cruel world we live in.'

Cassandra didn't know what to think about that. It didn't seem right, but it was the only world she knew. She saw Alexis and his mum hurrying across the sand, both laden with sacks of provisions.

'I thought you were sleeping!' she cried.

Alexis laughed. 'No! Didn't dad tell you?'

Daedalus stood up and apologised. 'I forgot that bit,' he admitted. 'I was too busy explaining about the oracle.' He turned to Cassandra and pointed out to sea. 'The demarch wants to get rid of us,' he said with a laugh. 'He doesn't want any more Athenian rioters trampling over his territory, so he has lent us that magnificent warship which you see rounding the point. Have a good look at it! It's equipped with a huge red sail and fifteen oars on either side.'

Cassandra stared at the enormous ship with its square red sail speeding across the waves in their direction. She looked up at Daedalus. 'But what about your own boat?' she asked. 'Surely you aren't going to leave it behind?'

Daedalus smiled. 'Don't worry about that. Our boat's going too. You'll see! They're going to lend us two more pairs of oars from their own ship and six of their oarsmen—that way, they reckon that we'll be able to keep pace with them, or not fall too far behind.

'And where are we headed?'

'Delos. After that, the demarch will be glad to get shot of us, so the captain of the warship will reclaim his oarsmen—and their oars—and we'll be on our own again.'

With the warship anchored offshore, Cassandra and her adopted family scrambled to collect their possessions—including the potter's wheel—and load them onto their boat. This done, they rowed out to the warship where helping hands reached out to secure their boat alongside. After that came the exchange of oars and oarsmen.

Daedalus and Hestia remained on their boat, to steer it and man the sail, assisted by a new crew of six oarsmen while Cassandra and Alexis soon found themselves comfortably seated in the stern of the larger vessel with nothing to do besides watch the mighty ship carve its way through the ocean. The ship already had its own helmsman, besides someone to man the sail, who sat idle as the sea lay becalmed.

'When do you think we will reach Delos?' Cassandra asked the helmsman, a small man with a brown leathery face and shifting inquisitive eyes.

'A couple of hours, I'd say,' he replied. 'Maybe more if the weather changes. There's not much to see there.'

Cassandra and Alexis exchanged glances. Then Cassandra said, 'We're heading for Crete, eventually. Is it far from Delos to Crete?'

As she correctly guessed, the man himself proved to be Cretan and her question provoked an excited response. 'Goodness!' he exclaimed. 'Crete's the place you want to go to! Knossos! That's where I was born. You'll find all the wonders of the world in that city—dancing, bull-leaping, pottery, wall-paintings, you name it...'

'I'm from Amnisos.'

'I know it. Nice place. On the coast—I've been there recently. A bit too close to the sea for my liking.'

Cassandra hesitated to ask the next question because of getting the answer she dreaded, but the man was already in full flow. 'There was that dreaded wave,' he said. 'I expect you were long gone before that time. I went there after the event and the wreckage was terrible to see—some of the buildings close to the sea were completely flattened. Still, most of the people survived, I'm glad to say.'

Alexis put his arm round her waist and gave her an encouraging smile.

At that moment, the wind got up and the helmsman had to adjust his tiller as the huge red sail responded to the change of direction.

'We'll soon be in Delos at this rate,' Alexis whispered.

'About another hour,' he agreed.

Alexis suddenly gave a cheerful laugh and said, 'You know, I've just realised something. It's my birthday! I'm thirteen years old today!'

The casual way he said it made Cassandra quite cross. 'How could you forget something as important as a birthday?' she asked.

'I don't know,' he said, looking out to sea, his dark hair blowing in the wind. 'There are good days and bad days. This is certainly a good day.'

'Yes, but it's still your birthday,' Cassandra insisted, 'and I want to give you something to remember it by.' She reached into her sack and produced the tiny chest pendant, which she pinned on his shirt.

He blushed and touched it with his finger. 'It's beautiful,' he said, 'but I have nothing to give you in return.'

She shook her head in frustration. This boy knew nothing about birthdays! 'You don't do that on birthdays!' she said. 'If it makes you feel any better, I have a pendant for your dad and another present for your mum.'

The helmsman had been listening to all this with amusement. 'She's just trying to tell you that she likes you. Just say 'thank you' and have done with it!' he advised Alexis.

'Thank you,' said Alexis.

CHAPTER THIRTEEN

They arrived at the island of Delos in the early afternoon. The warship anchored offshore and waited for the smaller craft to draw up alongside. Its captain had orders to return to Aegina before nightfall, so the air became full of shouted instructions as oars and crew were restored to their rightful places. Then the crew of the warship raised the anchor and turned the huge vessel around. Cassandra and Alexis and his family waved and shouted their thanks as they admired the departing ship with its square red sail and its oars dipped in harmony as they cut a furrow through the waves.

The island looked smaller than Cassandra had imagined and more primitive, judging by the small grey cottages dotted on the steep slope beyond the harbour. But a group of villagers soon descended the slope to greet them and surged forward to pull the boat onto the sand and attach it to its moorings. Their leader—a grizzled, red-faced veteran called Demosthenes—with a rich voice and rounded belly—seemed to be a popular figure among them. They laughed every time he spoke, even though Cassandra couldn't see anything funny in what he'd said. 'Welcome to Delos,' he cried 'The pearl of the Aegean!'—apologetic laughter. 'Our numbers may be few, but we know how to lay on a good show for visitors from far off lands'—more laughter—'You happen to have arrived on one of our festival days so, if you would kindly follow us up this hill, you will find dancing and wine a plenty and, after that, a place to lay your weary heads!'

Willing hands reached out to help them carry their baggage, and they mingled and chatted with the villagers as they set off up the slope. 'They are not used to visitors in these parts,' a tall girl who seemed, by her accent, to be a visitor too, whispered to Cassandra. 'But I like it here and I intend to stay.' Cassandra guessed her to be about sixteen years old and, judging by the jewels on her chiton, of aristocratic parentage. She reminded her a bit of Alethea except for the earnest expression in her eyes.

'My name is Sophia, which means wise,' said the girl, 'though truth to tell, I'm rubbish at mathematics, so wise can't mean the same as brainy.' She took Cassandra's arm in hers as they strode up the hill. 'And you are Cassandra, which means born with the gift of prophesy. I'm from Athens, you see, and I've heard everything about you.'

'So why...?'

'Why did I come to Delos? Because this island is sacred. It's the birthplace of Apollo and Artemis. But I noticed that it had no oracle!' She laughed and wagged a finger in front of Cassandra's nose. 'I know what you're thinking!' she said. 'Is Delos big enough to have an oracle?'

'It does seem quite small,' Cassandra admitted, looking at the few small houses scattered on the hillside.

'True,' Sophia agreed, 'but do you believe in visions?'

'I think so,' said Cassandra.

'Well, I had a vision that revealed that Delos will one day become the most sacred place in the Greek world.' She nudged Cassandra in the ribs and said, 'If you are a single woman and happy to remain that way, being an oracle is the best job you can get. It's hard work going into a trance, but it's very well rewarded!'

Cassandra thought that she did sound like Alethea, after all! 'I've spent some time at the Palace in Athens,' she said. 'I met a girl there called Alethea, who looked very similar to yourself. Do you happen to know her?'

Sophia gave her a wide-eyed stare and said, 'You should take my job and become a prophetess yourself! Alethea is my twin-sister! Our parents are both dead and we both struggle to assert our independence, but I hope I don't do it by lying and cheating like my dear sister!'

Cassandra breathed an inward sigh of relief. 'Actually, you're the very person I need to speak to,' she said. 'I came here to consult the oracle because--'

Sophia raised a hand to stop her in mid-flow. 'Don't say any more,' she insisted. 'Don't corrupt the message by telling me anything beforehand.

'Is it hard being a priestess?' asked Cassandra.

'Well, I can't say it's any fun going into a trance, and it requires hours of preparation, involving the use of medicines that might be considered harmful. But I seem to have a gift for it.'

Cassandra began to wonder if she had asked too much. Sophia seemed a nice person—very different from her twin sister. She didn't want to cause her any harm. 'My request is not so important,' she said.

'It doesn't need to be,' said Sophia. Visit me this evening at the mouth of the cave behind the temple and I will do my best to answer your questions.' She patted her hand and added, 'not too many, mind—or one tends to lose focus.'

They were interrupted by the sound of music, laughter, and voices raised in celebration. Cassandra realised that they'd arrived at the village square at the top of the hill. In a round space at the centre of the square, villagers danced to the sound of the lyre, the flute and the sistrum—a small metal device with a harsh rhythmic sound. The musicians sat on a bench at the edge of the space, clapping their hands at intervals to encourage the dancers. Behind them, tables were laid out all round the square, loaded with food and wine. Cassandra headed for the table on her right where Alexis and his mother shifted to make space for her.

At that moment, Demosthenes strolled over and tapped Daedalus on the shoulder. He pointed to one of the cottages lower down the slope. 'I might as well tell you this while I'm still sober,' he said. 'You never know what the evening may bring—but that is the house where you will be sleeping tonight.'

Alexis' parents thanked him many times over for his hospitality and stood up to follow his advice.

Keeping half an eye on the villagers, carrying tables, benches, and provisions into the village square, Demosthenes said, 'We have stowed the gear there which you gave us to carry, and you might seize this moment to stow the rest of your belongings there before the evening gets out of hand!' He shrugged. 'These festive occasions are, alas, too rare on our little island,' he said. 'So I hope you understand that we are all inclined to make the most of them.'

As they left, Sophia came over and tapped Cassandra on the shoulder. 'I'm going now to start my preparations,' she said. 'Apollo's temple is over there on your right. You'll see it as soon as you leave the square—and the cave is just behind. It will take me a couple of hours to prepare for your visit, but tread carefully because the night will be closing in by that time.'

'What was all that about?' asked Alexis.

When Cassandra explained about the oracle, he listened in his understanding way, but she sensed his uncertainty. Then she explained about Sophia and how different she was from the oracle in Delphi, whose predictions were dictated in advance by the rulers of Athens or Thebes. He nodded thoughtfully. Finally, he looked up and said, 'I get it! You need to know if your mother is still alive. That's the whole purpose of your journey! I'll go with you as far as the temple, at least.'

His parents soon returned, delighted with the lodgings arranged for them for that night. Cassandra told them about the priestess, and they listened and prayed for good news. Then they sat and ate, and watched the dancers and, after that, the comic performances of actors re-enacting the deeds of legendary heroes—Theseus appeared in one of them and Cassandra laughed with the rest of the spectators as he struggled to slay a minotaur the size of a cat. But her thoughts wandered as the evening drew on and she waited for the moment that might seal her future.

Then Alexis stood up and beckoned her to follow, and he led her in the semi-darkness to the nearby temple. 'I'll wait for you here,' he whispered. 'Just follow the light and you'll come to the cave.'

She saw the red glow that illuminated the arched entrance to the cave and smelt the incense that pervaded the air. And then out of nowhere she saw the prophetess herself—hardly recognisable as Sophia—just a powerful figure in a purple robe whose eyes shone with a strange mystical madness. 'You have come to consult the oracle,' announced the figure in a hollow voice. 'State your request!'

'I want to know if my mother is still alive,' said Cassandra in a clear voice.

She stood for several seconds watching the strange figure writhe in a mystic trance. Then the booming response echoed in the night air: 'Your mother escaped the great wave at Amnisos.

Seek and you will find her. But keep an open mind, lest you be disappointed by what you discover.'

After that, Cassandra bent and placed the five pieces of silver that the priestess had named as her fee on the plate at the entrance to the cave and re-joined Alexis who was waiting by the temple. She felt a surge of joy to hear it confirmed that her mother was still alive but disturbed by the idea of being disappointed.

'What could the Priestess mean by that?' she asked Alexis as they returned to the village square.

'You are used to thinking of your mother,' he suggested, 'as—well, not rich, but with money and a house. She lost most of that in the great wave. Maybe she found a job in the palace of Minos, painting walls and vases. Maybe she married again. But maybe she didn't. We must follow what leads we are given, but you must have a good understanding of your mother to know where to track her down.'

Cassandra felt humbled by Alexis' advice. He was right! Despite herself, she started to cry. Why hadn't she thought of this before? When you lose everything, it could be hard to get back on your feet and start again.

CHAPTER FOURTEEN

Cassandra and Alexis hurried down the slope. They wanted to leave early the next morning, so they'd planned to miss the rest of the festivities and head for an early night in the cottage. But as they passed the partygoers in the village square, Cassandra felt a sudden shiver of recognition. The noise had got louder and—among the loudest voices—she picked out accents that sounded harsh and rough and all too familiar.

She grabbed Alexis by the arm. 'Let's get out of here!' she whispered. 'The Mycenaeans have arrived. I even recognised one of them from the Palace.'

To Cassandra's surprise, when they opened the door of the cottage, they found Alexis' parents already packing the last of their possessions. 'We have to leave straightaway,' Daedalus said. 'I'll tell you all about it as soon as we get to that boat.'

She gave a sigh of relief. They had already spotted the danger! Those people she'd seen mingling with the village folk in the square were in full body armour. Would they never leave her alone? She grabbed her leather case and the small sack that held the last of her silver pieces and raced after Alexis and his parents, stumbling in the gathering darkness down the slope to the harbour.

Moored beside their little boat, a huge Mycenaean warship loomed out of the darkness like the one that had escorted them to Delos. But she knew this one wasn't there to help them.

Daedalus stepped onto their boat first and stood by the tiller, with arms outstretched to collect their baggage and stow it in the covered space at the stern. 'There's a good breeze tonight,' he said, 'So let's make an early start. It's a long way to Naxos, which is our last stop on the way to Amnisos and this gives us the best chance of getting there before that lot.' He pointed to the warship.

Cassandra sat beside Hestia at the tiller. 'Couldn't we punch a hole in that boat?' She asked. 'That would delay them a bit.'

Daedalus gave a rueful laugh. 'I wondered about that,' he said, 'but it might not delay them enough and then, if they caught us, they'd kill us.'

He was right, Cassandra thought as she sat and watched the wind catch the sail. Besides, with a breeze like this behind them, they might even be in Naxos before their pursuers could catch them. But Daedalus had said it would take them the best part of two days, so she knew this next part of the voyage wouldn't be easy.

Once they were safely out of the harbour, Daedalus sat with his back to them at the sail and told them what had happened earlier that night. 'We had just left the festivities,' he said, 'and returned to the cottage, reckoning to make an early night of it, when this Mycenaean knocked at our door.'

Cassandra remembered the face she had glimpsed the night before. Georgios! It had to be Georgios!

Daedalus adjusted the sail. 'Not a bad-looking fellow as Mycenaeans go,' he continued '—dressed in full armour but quite polite and presentable. His name was Georgios—I believe you know him, Cassandra?'

Yes, she knew him! Arete had warned her about him! She knew what he wanted!

'Anyway, he said he had no quarrel with us,' Daedalus said '—my family, he meant. We were free to continue our journey. But, as for you, Cassandra, your place was in Athens—to be educated at the palace, like your mother before you, and in time to become a suitable bride for one of the King's warriors.'

'Well, that's not going to happen!' said Hestia, giving Cassandra a sharp jab in the ribs.

'Go on!' said Cassandra. 'What did he say next?'

Daedalus laughed. 'He told me that the King's council had decided that Georgios himself should be the lucky bridegroom. He was quite nervous about telling us all this—to do him credit. I even began to feel sorry for the poor chap.'

Cassandra shuddered, but hearing the tone of amusement in Daedalus' voice, and the fact that she was sitting in a boat racing away from Delos, she could see that he'd done his best to make sure things didn't go the way Georgios wanted.

'So, what did I do?' asked Daedalus. 'I told him that you'd be happy to leave with him in the morning, at whatever time he wished—I didn't want him worrying about making an early start. And as soon as he left, we started to get packed for the next leg of our journey. I told Demosthenes about it. He was most amused by the plan!'

And here they were, thought Cassandra, sailing by the light of the moon, and making fair speed towards their destination. But would that be an end of it? She'd never expected the Mycenaeans to pursue her as far as Aegina, let alone Delos. What about Naxos? Would she ever be free of them?

As night fell, the breeze dropped. They had to resort to their oars and pressed ahead by the light of the moon. Daedalus sat beside his son on the rowing bench and Cassandra replaced him at the sail, catching what wind she could find. But for a long time, the sea lay becalmed, and the rowers strained at the oars until their arms ached while the boat barely inched forward. They realised that the progress they had made that night count-ed for little besides what a team of thirty rowers could achieve in a matter of hours.

Then they felt the first light patter of rain. And a few minutes later, out of the blackness, it came pelting down, drenching them all to the skin. They struggled around in their damp clothes, using what pots and pans they could find to bail out the water. And then—wonder of wonders!—Cassandra noticed that the wind that drove the storm had filled the sail and they were rocking along at an even fiercer pace than they'd achieved at the start of their journey—so fierce that Daedalus had to take over the sail and use all his strength to hold it in place.

After a while the storm abated, but to everyone's relief the breeze persisted, and Daedalus reckoned that they had covered more than a third of their journey. That gave them the slight edge—more so if you assumed that their pursuers were unlikely to be up before full daylight.

But Naxos seemed a long way off, when you were tired and hungry and sitting in damp clothes on a smallish boat, surrounded by a vast expanse of undulating waves. Cassandra leaned against Hestia's back and shut her eyes. She thought about Georgios, who seemed quite kind and polite when he'd led her into the audience chamber. That strange girl, Chloe, seemed happy to marry him, mainly because her parents approved the match and his farm lay next to theirs. But he'd changed his mind and chosen her—a girl of eleven—because she was the granddaughter of Poseidon. Did he even like her? It didn't seem to matter. He would pursue her to the ends of the earth because marrying her would make him look more important. Too bad for Georgios, she thought. He and his crew were probably still in bed while her little boat was nearly halfway to Naxos.

She didn't know how long she slept after that but, when she awoke, the light dazzled her eyes. She realised that the sea lay becalmed, and the family were taking a break in the pleasant warmth of the morning sun, checking their provisions, and chatting about the day that lay ahead. She noticed that it didn't take long for their clothes to dry out. Unfortunately, the same couldn't be said of the food. The bread had gone soggy and soaked in brine, the fruit had become squashed and inedible, and the milk had gone sour. They had to throw most of the food away—except for the milk, which they drank for their breakfast. 'We'll find plenty more food once we reach Naxos,' Hestia assured her. 'It's the largest island in the Cyclades.' That set them thinking about their destination.

Cassandra knew that heading for Naxos wasn't the quickest route to Amnisos. Daedalus had explained that the shorter western route would have meant skirting the volcanic island of Thera, where a new eruption could occur at any moment. Then, after Naxos, it was still a long way to Amnisos, but he reckoned that once they reached Cretan waters, they'd be safe from pursuit.

The breeze had returned, and Daedalus had his back to her, but she sensed his calm presence at the sail. Hestia sat beside her and Alexis on the other side. She felt squashed and uncomfortable, and badly in need of sleep, but she was happy to sit with half-closed eyes and watch the boat carve a furrow through the waves. She tried to forget about that little voice in her head, reminding her that she was tired and hungry. She had to focus all her thoughts on getting to Amnisos and starting the search for her mother.

CHAPTER FIFTEEN

After a while, the wind died down. The sail flapped idly in the still heat, and Alexis and his dad returned to the rowing bench. 'I reckon we're more than halfway there,' Daedalus announced, 'and Georgios and his crew will have only just started.'

'Poor Alexis!' Cassandra thought, seeing the set expression on his face as he struggled to match his father stroke for stroke. She didn't know much about Naxos apart from the fact that Zeus, the father of the Gods, was born there, and her own father, Theseus, had ditched Ariadne there, the Cretan princess who'd supposedly helped him against the minotaur. She wondered if that was before or after he met her mother. At that moment, she just thought of the island as a place where they might be able to get something to eat.

Daedalus tapped his son on the shoulder, and they rested their oars a moment. 'We should be in Naxos by early evening,' he announced, 'several hours in front of our pursuers, but that's not the end of our journey! We'll need all that time—not only to land unseen but to leave the island and head for Amnisos before they spot us and try to hunt us down.'

Cassandra half listened to his description of what they could expect to find in Naxos, pricking up her ears every time he mentioned the subject of food. Daedalus reckoned that Georgios would head for the main harbour in the west. The best way to avoid him would be to round the northern headland and moor in a sheltered cove he'd heard of on the east coast, too small for larger vessels. As for the islanders, they were Thracians, he thought, people from the east who—some said—were cannibals, but that was probably Athenian gossip. What worried him more was that the Mycenaeans had already settled in parts of the island, and with those people, you never knew...

It wasn't long before they spotted the northern tip of Naxos glinting in the early evening light. The wind had got up again and Daedalus attended to the sail while Hestia adjusted the tiller, so that the boat headed westward round the point, making a wide detour round the rocks that were known to lurk beneath the surface there. 'Demosthenes warned me about those rocks,' Daedalus confided.

At that moment, Cassandra spotted the red sail. She couldn't believe it at first. It was barely visible in the distance—just a tiny red square—she couldn't even see the boat, or the white foam stirred by the oars dipping in the waves. She didn't want to mention it. It had to be a mistake! But then the full body of the boat came into view. It had to be travelling at incredible speed. 'Quickly! Take down the sail!' She cried. 'I've seen them, but they may not have seen us.'

It was them, she realised. Georgios couldn't be fooled that easily. He'd have sensed a trick the moment Daedalus spoke of handing her over in the morning. It might have taken him some time to haul his crew away from the celebrations, but he'd set out later that night. Otherwise, he couldn't possibly have made up the distance they'd covered.

Daedalus had almost rounded the cape now. In a moment, that boat would be lost to view. Alexis and his dad leapt to the oars. 'There's one hope left for us,' Daedalus muttered. 'If we can't see them, they probably haven't seen us.'

As soon as they were clear of the rocks surrounding the cape, Daedalus dropped anchor at a point where he could observe the progress of their pursuers without fear of being seen.

'What will they do if they find us?' Cassandra asked.

'Don't ask!' Daedalus muttered. 'They will probably kill me and my family and take you back to Athens.'

Cassandra held her breath. She grabbed Hestia's arm and sat bolt upright at the stern, squeezing her eyes tight shut and praying with all her might that the worst thing in the world wouldn't happen. Then she heard Daedalus announce in a calmer voice, 'They have shifted direction. They're heading towards the main harbour on the other side of the island. It looks as if we're safe for the moment. They can't have seen us.'

'You did the right thing to warn us,' said Alexis. 'Removing the sail was a wise move.'

'Yes, quite the right thing!' Daedalus agreed. 'They might easily have spotted us.'

Cassandra felt a great rush of air come back to her lungs and glad that she hadn't been thought foolish. They were safe for the moment, Daedalus reckoned, but there was no saying what Georgios and his crew would decide to do next. With any luck, he would consider it a lost cause and head back to Athens. But he might well continue his pursuit until he approached the shores of Crete where Mycenaean craft were unwelcome. But he wouldn't set out again until the morning. After a night at sea, he'd have a mutiny on his hands if he asked them to repeat the ordeal. For themselves, it was a matter of life and death. They would have to moor in that harbour further up the coast and rest there until nightfall, then start the longest leg of their journey under the cover of darkness.

Happily, after they rounded the point, the wind got up again and Daedalus returned to the sail, which meant that Alexis was able to take his place at the stern and go to sleep. He needed that, Cassandra thought. He wasn't that much older than herself, but he behaved at times like a full-grown man. She lay back and began to relax. It seemed to take longer than she'd expected to reach that sheltered harbour that Daedalus had talked about. Such a long time! But at least they were safe for the moment. She felt her eyelids beginning to close...

When she opened them again, she realised that she must have dropped off for a long time because it felt like surfacing from a dark tunnel of dreams. She marvelled at how the family managed. Alexis and his dad hardly seemed to sleep at all. The first thing she noticed was that her prop had gone, because she'd grown so used to leaning on Hestia's shoulder that she nearly lost her balance without it. Instead, she looked up and saw Hestia standing on a patch of rocky soil where the boat lay moored. She dimly remembered what Daedalus had said about a sheltered cove and realised this must be it. She looked up at the overarching rocks and saw why Daedalus had chosen this spot to hide. 'Where are the others?' she asked.

'They've gone to search for food,' Hestia said with a smile. 'You've been asleep for a while. I wish I could do that, believe me!'

At that moment, Cassandra looked to her right and saw a narrow, muddy stairway patched with rough stones spiralling upwards towards the land above.

'What are you doing?' Hestia asked.

'I thought I might join them,' Cassandra said, with her foot on the first step.

'Well, don't!' Hestia said, in a cross voice, grabbing her by the shoulders. 'You don't think we've come all this way to keep you safe, just for you to wander off like a headless chicken and get captured by one of these Mycenaean soldiers! They're all over the place, I tell you—not just the men from the boat, but locals too.'

This was the first time Cassandra had heard Hestia get cross, and it made her feel miserable. She knew what it meant for this family to sacrifice their own safety and comfort to bring her all this way, just to protect her from danger. She threw her arms round Hestia and buried her face in her ample bosom. 'I'm sorry, Hestia,' she sobbed. 'It was thoughtless of me.'

'There, there, little chicken,' Hestia murmured, stroking her hair. 'Think no more of it. You'd better dry your eyes now, because I think I can hear 'the boys' returning.'

Father and son arrived at the bottom of the steps looking worn and hopeless. 'It's no good,' Daedalus said. 'The land around here is barren, and as soon as you step further inland, you can see Mycenaeans—locals, probably. They may be harmless, they may not, but there is always the risk of word getting round where we're hiding. I know how hungry we all are, but we can fast for a day or two without coming to any serious harm. I think we'd better leave this place and head for the open sea again.'

'Do you think they've found us already?' asked Alexis. He pointed to a boat very similar to their own heading across the ocean from the east towards the cove where their boat was moored.

Daedalus hesitated. 'It looks Cretan to me,' he said. 'And it's way too small to be theirs. What's more, there's just a man and a young boy on board, so I fancy they could be harmless.'

As the boat drew closer, they could see that it was smaller than their own—small enough for the old man to manage the pair of oars, while the boy sat at the stern with his hand on the tiller. The empty space was piled high with provisions.

'A trader!' said Daedalus with excitement. 'We'd better be careful about this!' he whispered. He climbed back into their boat and the others followed. 'He's probably a local—which means he'll stop off at every harbour. We'd better not let him see how much we're in need of his goods, or he may raise his prices. And on no account must we tell him where we're heading, or the rest of the island will soon get to know about it.'

'Where else could we be heading?' asked Alexis.

'Samos. Let's say Samos—that's just east of here. I have a brother there, or I can say I have.'

The old man smiled at Daedalus as he moored alongside. Daedalus returned his smile.

That was a good start, Cassandra thought, her eyes lingering on the goods on display; fresh bread, milk, honey, grapes, peaches, melons...

'You're lucky!' said the old man with a crafty smile. 'I'm from Samos, and I always start my sales here before rounding the headland towards the west coast where most of my business is done. Where are you heading?' he asked.

'Mykonos,' said Daedalus, quickly adapting his story.

'And where would you be from?'

'Oh, Ithaca originally, but that's a long story.'

'So, I suppose you might be interested in taking home some of my wares?'

Cassandra held her breath. The boy had said nothing up to this point, but she could see from the smile on his face that the old man knew more than he was letting on. He must have wondered why they were moored in this isolated cove instead of the west coast where markets would be plentiful.

Daedalus inspected the bread and the milk, which looked fresh enough, and the fruit on display, and ordered enough for the four of them. Then the haggling began. The first price that the old man proposed was ten times the going rate. And he didn't seem prepared to go much lower. 'It's a seller's market,' he said.

Cassandra thought Daedalus was too polite for his own good. You had to look at the numbers! That was how you settled things on the playground. 'Look,' she whispered in Daedalus' ear, 'There's four of us, and two of them—or one and a half really', she added, taking another look at the boy. 'Why don't you just pay him a fair price and threaten to push him overboard if he won't accept it?'

Daedalus blinked and nodded. He leaned over and seized the man by the throat and said, 'Look! You're a dishonest rogue and you're trying to take advantage of us. I could take your goods for nothing if I wanted. Instead, I'm a reasonable man so I'm prepared to pay you half what you asked for and I'll take the goods' straightaway'—which he proceeded to do—'and you'd better leave without another word, because I'm sorely tempted to drown you.'

That was more like it, Cassandra thought, though she couldn't see why Daedalus needed to be so generous. She quickly reached into her sack and slipped her remaining bits of silver into his hand to help with the purchase. Then they sat and watched the man sail away, knowing that he would soon be increasing his earnings by informing the rest of the island of their presence.

But the food was too good to be missed. So, before they set off on their final journey, they settled down to what turned out to be their last banquet at sea.

CHAPTER SIXTEEN

So, what could they do, with no land in sight, but row through the night—or sail with a favourable wind—for another day and another night until the dawn of the following day when the shores of Crete loomed out of the morning mist, and they knew they were safe from pursuit.

Cassandra woke with these memories hammering in her mind, but couldn't find the energy to stir from where she lay in the warm sand. They'd arrived close to where her former home had stood, a short walk away from the harbour town of Amnisos, which she knew was a good thing, but she was starving—they all were—and that seemed all that mattered. She looked at their few belongings scattered around them—the cases of clothes and treasured possessions that they'd struggled to carry up the slope from the boat. At that moment, she'd have been happy to sell anything she owned for a single loaf of bread.

Daedalus was the next to awake, and she admired the way he managed to shake himself and rise to his feet. He even managed a smile. 'I've got a plan!' he said, producing a card from his sleeve. 'I'm off to see the potter we met at the market in Colona. I have his address here. I won't be long.' She felt sad for him, seeing him stumble across the sand, knowing how hungry he must feel—and stiff too, after all that rowing. Then she looked across at Alexis, still flat on his back, sleeping. It must have been doubly hard for him, struggling to match his father stroke for stroke. Hestia had taken his place at the oars from time to time, but she admitted that she couldn't keep pace with her husband.

Cassandra had learned something from this family, she thought—the way they soldiered on without complaining when life got tough. That made her think of her mother and the words of the oracle. How would she have coped after standing at the top of that slope, watching her house and everything she owned vanish beneath the waves? It was no use assuming that she was living comfortably as before. What if she'd been forced to find work as a servant or even a slave?

These gloomy thoughts were interrupted by the sight of Alexis opening his eyes and struggling to get used to his new surroundings. He made two attempts to stand up, then rolled on his front and used his hands to raise himself into an upright position. He staggered for a bit, then lay down again. 'It's no use, Cassandra,' he confessed with a rueful laugh. 'I can't do it. Maybe later...'

'Stay where you are,' she whispered, stroking his hair. 'I think your dad's gone to get food.' It was a wish more than a certainty, but it seemed to satisfy him because he smiled and fell asleep again.

She must have fallen asleep herself for an hour or more because she felt the sun scorching her face when she sat up and noticed Alexis' dad returning down the slope. He had a sack over his shoulder and a face bursting with good news. Hestia awoke at the sound of his voice and sat up with a beam of expectation on her round face. Then Alexis too struggled into a sitting position and looked around, wondering what the fuss was about. As soon as he saw the expression on his dad's face, he gave a cry of joy. 'You've brought food, dad, haven't you?' he exclaimed.

'I've brought more than that,' said his dad, sitting cross-legged on the sand and dumping the sack at his feet. 'But let's eat first, and afterwards I'll tell you my great bit of good news.'

Daedalus extracted a cloth from the sack and carefully laid upon it four loaves of bread, four sealed jars of milk, goat's cheese, melons, and grapes. 'Go carefully,' Alexis' mum advised. 'So much food in one go can do harm to an empty stomach.' Everyone nodded at her words, but Cassandra doubted if anyone followed her advice—let alone Cassandra herself.

An hour later, when their glazed and sleepy faces suggested that the meal was over, Daedalus sprang upon them his item of good news. 'I went first to the harbour,' he said. 'And I managed to sell our boat at a good price—well, I figured we wouldn't be needing it after this! And there's a great shortage of boats there, since so many were destroyed by that wave.'

They all raised a cheer. Cassandra saw the relief on Hestia's face and guessed how much this meant in terms of restoring the family finances. But Daedalus hadn't finished yet. In his polite way, he looked a bit put out at being interrupted in full flow. He coughed and waited for their full attention before saying, 'Then I went straightway to Hermes the potter—'

'Is that the nice man we met in Colona?' asked Hestia.

'Yes, yes. He's a wonderful fellow and generous to a fault. The fact is that his business is expanding, and he's desperately short of skilled staff. He's keen to employ Hestia, a glazer, and myself as a potter, and he's even offered us temporary accommodation in his house.'

'That's wonderful!' exclaimed Hestia. She got up and gave him a hug. 'I can't believe you've achieved all this,' she said. 'After all that rowing and all those sleepless nights!'

Daedalus didn't seem to mind being interrupted this time. 'You should see the place!' he continued. 'It's called the 'House of Lilies'. It's on two storeys, with about ten rooms, a courtyard, a place where you can wash and frescoes on most of the walls! It was easy enough to find. It towers above the other houses in the neighbourhood.'

Cassandra had begun to think that so much good news was almost as hard to digest as the food she'd just eaten, when Daedalus tapped her on the shoulder and said, 'and my final piece of news is for you, Cassandra. Your mother was last seen a few days after the disaster, heading for Knossos.'

Cassandra felt a sudden thrill of nervous excitement. Knossos wasn't so far away. She might even walk there the very next morning.

'I have kept the details of the lady who last saw her,' Daedalus said, 'so that you can visit her tomorrow before you and Alexis make the journey. It's only a short walk along a paved road to Knossos, so you'll be able to get there and back in a day. Maybe your mother will be with you! Let's hope so! If not, we'll have to plan the next move.'

Cassandra had sudden doubts. Her mother might be in Knossos! But what if she weren't? Finding her there would make her job ten times harder. That city was enormous!

The effect of so much good food had only made her feel sleepier. She noticed it had the same effect on Alexis and his mum, who sat there looking worn out. She felt sorry for Alexis' dad who had done so much in a short time to retrieve their fortunes. But he didn't seem to mind. He just looked up and smiled at their sleepy faces. 'We've been invited to my friend's house for dinner,' he said, 'but what we all need now is sleep, so I suggest that we lie here in the sun for a while and wake in time to walk the short distance to my friend's house.'

Cassandra lay back in the warm sand and felt her eyes closing again. She imagined herself meeting her mother in Knossos at the gates of the palace. She suddenly realized, to her surprise, as she counted the days since her flight on the angel's back, that less than three weeks had passed. So, her mother wouldn't look much older than when she'd last seen her racing back up the sand, with Lycos not far behind. She had the sort of face anyone would want to remember, so maybe she wouldn't be so hard to find if you simply asked around.

She opened her eyes and looked around her. She didn't know why she felt so sleepy. She'd managed to sleep much more than the family over the course of their journey. It must be all that food, she decided, after all that time without eating. She closed her eyes and thought of her mother again, just as she'd been when she saw that tsunami. Her mother was speaking to her now. 'Get your sandals!' she cried. 'We have to make a dash for it!' She stared at the huge wave thundering towards her. Then, out of nowhere, that angel towered over her again. What was he doing standing there on the sand? 'I've come to take you back to Athens,' he said. 'Poseidon is angry with you. This time you won't escape a whipping.'

'No way!' she protested. 'I'm not going back there.'

'You don't have a choice.'

Cassandra awoke with a start. *Could he do that*? She wondered. These gods had the power to do whatever they wanted. If he'd sent a messenger to fly her to Athens, why couldn't he do it again? And why hadn't she thought of that before? That would have made their whole journey pointless. She looked round and saw that Alexis and his parents were still sleeping. She'd ask Daedalus about that angel, she decided. It didn't bear thinking about. Poseidon seemed a long way off at that moment. She lay back in the soft sand, put the cloth over her eyes to shield them from the sun and let herself drift into sleep again.

She must have slept for hours, she thought, when she felt the hand of Alexis on her shoulder and sat up and looked around her, feeling wide awake for the first time in days. She saw his dad stumbling around, struggling to smarten himself up for their visit to the potter's house.

She noticed Alexis' mum appearing from a small wooden hut at the top of the slope where she'd gone for a change of clothes. She carried her old clothes in a sack as she returned down the slope. Cassandra thought she'd do the same. But more than anything, she needed to wash. Alexis and his dad already looked washed and ready to go, she noticed. Then Alexis stooped and placed a bucket of sea water at her feet. 'That's all we used,' he said. 'Take your case, and I'll carry this bucket up to the hut for you.'

Finally, they stood together beside their sacks and cases, mainly full of unwashed clothes, laughing and admiring one another's efforts to make themselves presentable for the visit to the potter's house. Then Cassandra opened her hand and revealed the two tiny objects she'd retrieved from her case, while washing and changing her clothes in the hut at the top of the slope. She showed Alexis' mum the tiny golden earrings and helped attach them to her ears and she pinned the golden chest pin onto his dad's white over-garment, or 'himation'. Then, in the best of spirits, they set off up the slope towards the potter's house.

Cassandra grabbed Daedalus' arm and told him about what she'd just dreamed about the angel. 'Could he really take me back to Athens?' she asked.

Daedalus laughed. 'Funnily enough, if you'd asked me that a week ago,' he said, 'it might well have happened. But I remember Demosthenes telling me that King Cecrops recently launched a competition among the Olympian gods for the prize of becoming the patron god or goddess of Athens.'

'And who won?'

'Well, the chief contenders were Poseidon and Athene, and the prize went to Athene. Poseidon was furious! He felt he'd been cheated. So, no! He won't be sending anyone to Athens again—especially not his granddaughter!'

CHAPTER SEVENTEEN

Hermes, the potter, and his wife, Aspasia, stood on the steps of their villa to greet them. Hermes was a big man. His whole body radiated energy and enthusiasm, softened by the humorous twinkle in his eyes. Aspasia—who only reached up to his chin—was a shy, attractive woman who stole occasional glances at her husband before speaking.

Hermes did most of the talking. 'Come in, come in!' he insisted, greeting each of them in turn with a hug. 'I know you must be hungry, but first I must show you my house—well, at least the bits that will interest you as fellow potters and glazers. You see the courtyard below? Have you noticed the colourful mosaics? My wife, Aspasia, did that—didn't you, darling?' He placed his hand over her shoulder, and she smiled and gave a modest blush.

'Now we must go up these steps,' he announced. 'It's the second floor that will interest you most. Here are your sleeping quarters and—Ah yes! Cassandra! This is the room you need to see!' He squeezed her arm and asked, 'Do you see that lovely fresco that covers more than half the wall?'

Cassandra gazed in wonder at the free-flowing design that almost covered the entire wall. She admired the arrangement of red and white lilies—and mint too, and irises and papyrus, all artfully placed in their separate pots! What artistry! What grace!

'People call this 'The House of the Lilies' you know,' she heard Hermes saying. 'Your mother painted that fresco! A lovely lady, your mother, and a talented artist too—I wish she'd stayed, but she had to follow her husband—Lycos, wasn't that his name? Hm...'

Cassandra felt a thrill run through her body at the thought that her mother had been in that very room not so long ago. She knew her mother was an artist, but it made her proud to feel that she could paint a fresco like that. The mention of Lycos worried her. She had never liked him, but if an adult like Hermes seemed to have doubts about him, that meant something. Why did her mother need to follow him? This place would have been perfect for her! She followed Hermes into the next room. He was talking to Alexis now. He had a hand on his shoulder. 'I like this lad!' he announced to the room at large. 'I can see he's a good fellow! I noticed that in Colona—the way he looks after his young lady.'

Cassandra felt pleased for Alexis. He just smiled in his modest way, but he deserved that compliment. It reminded her of how he'd rescued her on the Acropolis. He might have liked to stay in that house and practise his trade as a potter, but instead he would follow her to Knossos and beyond that if need be.

Hermes had begun to seat them all at the long dining table. He was good at that sort of thing, Cassandra noticed. He had a quick understanding of people and knew how to make them feel at ease. He'd placed Alexis on his right hand, and herself next to his wife on his left. She realised that he'd done that because she and Alexis would be leaving the next day and he wanted to get to know them. She noticed a space on her left side and Aspasia whispered, 'that's for the surprise guest, the lady who travelled with your mother to Knossos. She'll be going with you tomorrow. I know you'll like her.' Aspasia patted her on her shoulder and turned to speak to her husband.

Cassandra looked up and saw a young lady hurrying into the room, gasping her apologies. She looked younger even than Cassandra's mother and Cassandra felt instantly attracted to her warm, honest face, knowing this was just the sort of person that her mother would have liked. You couldn't call her exactly pretty, but her eyes were alive with understanding. You knew you could talk to that sort of person, she thought, and she would listen and try to help.

The dishes came and went, but Cassandra hardly noticed what she ate. She only had eyes and ears for the woman who eased into the seat beside her. 'I'm Cressida' said the young woman, adding with a laugh, 'My parents gave me that name because it means gold, but it seems to have escaped me somehow. And you're Cassandra, I know. Your mother told me so much about you.'

'Did she know—'

'That you were rescued by an angel?' Cressida replied, giving her a quick look, as if reading her thoughts. 'She saw that. It was the one thing that kept her going. She dreamed of following you to Athens—she knew that's where the angel would take you—it being your father's city.' She saw the worried look on Cassandra's face and said, 'Don't worry, she didn't make that journey. She had to follow Lycos to Knossos.'

'Knossos?'

'Yes. He went ahead, saying he'd meet her there at the entrance to the Palace. It was I that went with her to Knossos, hoping to track him down.'

Cressida stopped talking and patted Cassandra on the hand. 'I say it's a bit rude of us to go on chattering like this,' she said, 'and ignoring the other guests. Besides, I've noticed you haven't even finished what's on your plate. We'll have plenty of time tomorrow to talk on the road to Knossos when we go with—Alexis, isn't that his name?' She smiled in his direction and raised her glass to him, and he quickly responded.

Cassandra felt happy to remain silent for the rest of the meal, surrounded by a sea of friendly faces and mulling over all that Cressida had told her. It had never even crossed her mind that her mother would have tried to track her down in Athens. But that would be the obvious thing to do once she'd seen her rescued by that angel. Cassandra looked across at Hermes. Her mother should never have bothered about Lycos—the moment he went ahead to Knossos, she should have known he meant to give her the slip and she'd never be able to track him down. She should have accepted Hermes's offer and stayed on at The House of the Lilies. Hermes would have given her the support she needed—she could have earned good money painting and glazing. But her mother should have searched for her in Athens—except it was lucky she didn't, because it was the worst place to be at this time. It was all so confusing that she gave up thinking about it.

The dishes came and went and, as the evening drew on, Cassandra felt herself beginning to drown in a sea of cheerful banter, but it was a comfortable sort of drowning, among laughing, friendly faces, where you knew help lay close at hand. She saw Cressida chatting with Alexis' parents and turned to notice Aspasia, who had risen from the table and held out a hand to help raise her to her feet. 'Come on, dear,' she whispered. 'It's getting late, and you have to make an early start tomorrow.'

Cassandra stopped to thank Hermes for a wonderful evening and followed her along the corridor to the bedroom, where Aspasia explained, 'There are two beds in that room. The other bed is for Cressida, who will be joining you shortly.'

CHAPTER EIGHTEEN

It was Cressida that woke her the next morning, standing over her bed, fully dressed, and placing a glass of milk in her hand. 'Will that do you for the moment?' she asked. 'Alexis'—as you call him—is already up and it will be good to make an early start before the formalities of breakfast delay our journey.' She laughed—'Well, I like breakfast, especially in this house, but we can easily get something to eat along the way.'

Cassandra washed and dressed in a matter of minutes, with the sack over her shoulder holding the silver pieces that Alexis' dad had given her for their journey. She found Alexis and Cressida waiting outside the entrance to the villa and was happy at first to walk behind them in the morning half-light, as Cressida told him what she remembered from her earlier trip. 'We never found Lycos,' she explained. 'He took some of your mother's jewels with him—he said he needed them to pay for their lodgings—so I didn't expect to find him.'

'Maybe be didn't stay in Knossos,' suggested Alexis.

'Exactly. He might easily have headed off in a different direction—along the coast, perhaps. After all, he was a fisherman. So, when he told her to meet him in Knossos, that was probably the last place you'd expect to find him.'

Cressida turned and gave Cassandra a hug. 'I'm sorry, Cassandra,' she exclaimed. 'Here am I talking to your friend and leaving you out of it, when you should be walking with us on either side and you in the centre. After all, it's your mother we're looking for. Look, we've reached the highway now, so let's walk three abreast and work out what to do when we arrive in the city.'

Cassandra paused in wonder at the magnificent paved road, walled off from the surrounding countryside by a low line of carved rectangular stones. She felt like a princess stepping into the middle of that road with her two friends on either side.

Alexis wanted to know whether Cassandra's mother had applied for a job at the palace. 'After all, she was a skilled artist,' he said.

Cressida hesitated. 'That's what I told her.' She said, 'but it's a huge place, the palace, run on strict, bureaucratic lines. You've got to know the right people, or at least be wearing the right clothes to even be considered for a job.' She squeezed Cassandra's shoulder and explained, 'Your poor mother was still wearing the clothes she wore when she escaped from the waves. I offered to buy her new ones. It was the least I could do, though I didn't have much money at the time. I'm not talented like your mother and I was only working as a chambermaid.'

'And she refused your offer?' asked Alexis.

Cressida shrugged. 'Well, you know what these artists are like! She thought appearances didn't matter. It was only her art that counted. Besides, she didn't like to borrow from a friend.'

'But did she apply for a job at the palace?' asked Alexis.

'Yes, and they turned her away at the entrance. That's the way with these officials. Appearances are all that count!'

Cassandra recognised this picture of her mother, and it made her sad. She was so young and beautiful and used to having it all. She couldn't stoop to borrowing from a friend or wearing smart clothes just to be offered a job painting frescoes. 'Did she apply for work with local potters?' she asked Cressida.

'She tried a few of those but was probably refused for the same reasons.'

They walked along in silence for a bit.

'Did my mum know that I'd escaped from Athens?' Cassandra asked.

Cressida gave her a surprised glance. 'Everyone knew! Well, she'd met Hermes, hadn't she? He knew where you were heading.'

Cassandra had a hollow feeling in her stomach. 'But if she knew...' she began.

Cressida put an arm round her shoulder. 'Yes, if she knew, how were you expected to find her? I told her that—she needed to leave an address—but it must have slipped her mind.'

'Well, it's up to us to do the finding!' said Alexis, trying to make light of the matter. 'Hm. So where do we start?'

'Well, it's a huge city,' said Cressida—'the biggest by far in the Greek world. There are reckoned to be one hundred thousand people living in Knossos and its surroundings. We can start with the palace. Who knows? She might have tried again and been lucky—or someone might remember her face and know where she was heading.'

'What about the potteries?' asked Cassandra.

'Yes, someone seeking a job might remember seeing a like-minded soul on the same mission. Sooner or later, we'll meet someone who remembers her and knows where she was heading.'

Despite herself, Cassandra felt encouraged by that reasoning. You just had to ask and ask, and in the end, you'd find that tiny clue that helped you to find her. She had something of her own to add to the search because she remembered what her mother was like, how she loved to wander through the streets of Amnisos and stop and stare at beautiful objects, like certain trees or flowers, or buildings or sometimes objects seen in potters' yards.

'What are you thinking about?' asked Alexis.

She told him, and Cressida agreed that this was something they had to bear in mind. In her experience, Cassandra's mother liked to wander—and her wanderings might end up in unexpected places. Alexis shook his head in doubt. He wondered if this information would make it any easier to find her.

They were approaching the city now. In front of them, they could see a vast paved square. At the edges of the square, tradesmen had set up their stalls, selling anything from drinks and hot food to pottery and cheap ornaments. In the centre of the square, they saw officials and visitors pass in either direction, entering or leaving the palace which loomed high on their right.

'The palace first,' suggested Cressida. 'I think it's best if Cassandra handles this one. A young girl on her own, looking for her mother, is more likely to receive a hearing. Alexis and I will sit on this stone bench and wait. Good luck, Cassandra!'

Cassandra walked through the open entry gates and found herself in another large space facing an inward curving wall of entry booths. The booths closest to the central archway, she guessed by the length of the queues, were for visitors. The same visitors would leave the palace through the open archway. It was the booths at the sides that interested Cassandra. Here it was a question of studying the faces of the officials and judging the one that might be sympathetic to her request. She picked on a motherly lady in one of the right-hand booths who had just finished dealing with an elderly customer and raced to the booth before anyone else could take his place.

'I am looking for my mother,' she cried, somewhat breathlessly.

'Oh dear!' said the lady, peering down from her booth. 'How old are you?'

'I'm eleven.'

'And how long ago since you last saw her?'

'The lady I'm staying with saw her a week ago.'

The lady gave her a smile of encouragement. 'That's good then. At least you have someone to help you.'

'Yes. My mother came here seeking a job as a painter and glazer. She'd already painted a fresco at the House of Lilies in Amnisos.'

'Hold on, dear. I'll get some assistance.'

The lady closed the square door to the opening of her booth, leaving Cassandra to stand there for a few minutes, tense with expectation. Then the door opened again, and a tight-lipped lady with expensive earrings and a narrow face stared down at her with an air of distaste. 'I do remember your mother,' she said. 'She came here a week ago, seeking a job in our fresco department. I told her she was unsuitable, and that was the end of it. I am sorry I can't help you any further.'

'You haven't helped me at all,' said Cassandra, hurrying off to re-join her friends on the stone bench.

'Never mind,' said Cressida. 'We were expecting that, but we had to give it a try. Alexis has been enquiring about potteries.'

'There's a whole street lined with them,' Alexis said. 'It's just up there on our right!'

They hurried through the crowd and stared in wonder at a wide, paved avenue lined on either side with potters' yards stretching up the hill and out of sight.

'What do you think, Cassandra?' asked Cressida. 'Would your mother have visited these yards?'

'Definitely.'

'All of them?'

Cassandra had to think for a bit. 'She'd have been more interested in the ones working on frescoes,' she said, 'or the ones offering employment, but she'd probably stop and chat to anyone with a friendly face, so I don't know where to start.'

Cressida looked at her with amusement. 'I think you've nailed it, Cassandra,' she said. 'Frescoes, job offers and friendly faces. We've got a long day ahead of us, so let's have something to eat in that café across the road and then get started. And while we're about it, let's book rooms there for tonight. We need an address where she can find us if she gets to hear we're searching for her.'

CHAPTER NINETEEN

A lexis said they needed a system. He noted that the first building on the left, where they were standing, was numbered one and the last building on the opposite side was numbered two hundred and eighty-seven, which meant they had nearly three hundred buildings to check. He'd check the first ten buildings on the left, and Cassandra and Cressida could check the first ten on the right, conferring together the moment any of them hit on a positive response. Cassandra had secret doubts about Alexis' system. That's what Alexis would do, she imagined. He'd stop at every potter's yard and go on to the very end, if that's what it took to secure a job. She had to admit she doubted if her dear mum had quite that stamina.

Alexis had got to number six when he beckoned them across the road to join him. 'I was telling this young man about a young lady who came seeking a job painting and designing frescoes,' said the elderly potter, who answered two of Cassandra's requirements—frescoes and a friendly face. 'I'd have liked to say 'yes,'' he said—'her being so young and in need of employ-ment, but not having a vacancy, I suggested she try number thirty-eight. I knew the potter there had a vacancy.'

'Had the lady got long dark hair?' asked Cassandra.

'That's the one! And a nice voice. I remember that.'

'That was my mum.'

'I'll remember that. I saw her a couple of days ago. If I see her again, I'll let her know to look out for you. May I know where you'll be staying?'

'At the café on the corner,' said Cassandra, thanking the man, and following Cressida across the road to continue their search.

No luck on their side and no luck on the next twenty build-ings they tried, though Alexis had two more 'hits' directing him to building thirty- eight.

'I'm beginning to see a pattern here,' Cressida whispered to Cassandra. 'All the 'hits' have been on Alexis' side. I reckon that means your mum just continued up that side of the road until she found what she wanted—in which case, let's cross the road and join him.'

They stood with Alexis outside building thirty-eight. There were a few pots on display and a solitary, well-executed fresco depicting a fisherman dangling his catch in either hand. The man that came to the door didn't look that promising either, though he was handsome in his way. He had a well-weathered face with a scar on one cheek, and he stood in the doorway and asked 'Can I help you?' in a voice that suggested helping people wasn't his speciality.

'We're looking for Callista,' said Cressida in a firm voice.

'Oh yea, who's she?'

'She's my mum,' said Cassandra.

'Yea, well, I did see her, but she wasn't right for the sort of work I had in mind.'

'Doing frescoes?'

'Yea, she did do a fresco, but I wanted other stuff doing too—something in the marketing line, and she wasn't up for that.'

The door slammed and, at that moment, the next door opened, and a thrill of hope ran through her veins. Somehow, Cassandra knew what would happen next. A youngish man with a kind face appeared at the door and said, 'Don't worry about that man! He'll be gone from that place soon. They're taking him to prison where he belongs. If you're looking for your mum, you'd better come inside. She's longing to see you!'

Cassandra hesitated. She suddenly realised that she'd got it all wrong. She thought of what the priestess had said and saw that she'd expected too much. The number 39 on the door said it all. They'd been foolish looking on the other side of the street. Her mum wouldn't have thought of looking that far. The idea of her mother that she'd formed in her absence from her desperate desire to see her and know that she was still alive was like a shiny puzzle, and now she could see all the pieces fall apart. Her mum hadn't followed her to Athens as she'd wanted to do, though she could have sold her jewels to pay for the journey. And she hadn't really made much effort to find her. She hadn't even bothered to leave an address where she could be found. She'd walked a few miles to Knossos and looked for a job, but she hadn't tried that hard. She was like those girls in the palace, just used to doing what they were told. She'd been married—if you could call it that—at the age of fourteen. She'd always had a man at her side. Cassandra felt an unbearable love for her, but knew she couldn't live this way, following her around and being dependent on others. She'd see her every day—she'd love that—but she'd need space to grow up on her own.

She looked up and saw the man smiling down at her from the top of the steps. 'Well, aren't you going to come inside?' he asked.

'I'm sorry,' she said in a rush. 'You took me by surprise. I'll just have a word with my friends.' She ran down the steps and whispered to Cressida, 'Keep my room. I'll be back in a bit.' Cressida seemed to understand, but Alexis gave a puzzled frown.

She found her mother waiting in the bedroom and shed tears of love as she lay on the mattress, safely snuggled in her mother's arms. 'I have missed you so much!' her mother whispered in her ear. 'I have searched for you everywhere. I thought I might never see you again. Can you imagine?'

But the more her mother spoke, the more Cassandra felt bitter thoughts come creeping into her mind. She remembered Alexis and his family who'd risked their lives, crossing the ocean for her sake and Brontës, who'd died defending her.

'You've gone quiet,' her mother said, sitting up but still holding her on her lap. 'What are you thinking?'

'I want to go back to Amnisos.'

'What? You're leaving me?'

The words came in a rush. 'No, I love you. I want to see you every day,' she insisted, 'but there's this boy I know who helped rescue me from the Palace in Athens. And his family left their home at the risk of their own lives to ferry me across the waters to Crete. And they did all this to help me find you, not knowing if you were alive. And now they are living in the House of Lilies where you painted that beautiful fresco. And the mother paints frescoes there too, and the father is a potter. And the boy wants to be a potter too and I want to help him.'

Her mother looked thoughtful and sad. 'I know I've not been a good mother,' she said.

'I love you,' Cassandra repeated, giving her a hug 'and I hope you will let me see you every day and still do all those nice things we used to do together, but I want to stay in Amnisos and learn a trade and give something back to this family too, who have sacrificed so much for me.'

Her mother nodded and stood up. 'Well, you are a wise girl,' she said. 'And brave too. I wish I'd been like that at your age. I think you have come to a good decision, and I don't expect you to make this walk every day so long as we can always stay in close touch.'

Her mum went to the door and exchanged words with her partner who smiled and wished her well, as she left the house and walked to the café on the corner to re-join her friends. She felt glad to see that her mum had found a kind partner at last—a person who looked as if he could be trusted. But she didn't feel needed in this set-up.

Alexis looked surprised at her decision—as well he might be, she thought—having done so much to help her. But when she explained that her quest was really at an end because her mother was alive and had got all that she'd ever wanted—a kind partner to share her life with—he began to understand. As for herself, Cassandra explained, she would always stay in touch with her mother, but she wanted to stay with her adopted family at the House of Lilies—if that were possible—and learn to become a potter like himself. Then Alexis grinned and gave her a contented hug. Cressida looked on and smiled. 'Having met your mother—a lovely lady, for all her faults—' she said, 'I think you've made a very sensible choice.'

GREEK QUIZ

*F*orm as many English words as you can from the following Greek roots.

A lot of English words derive from Anglo-Saxon, Latin and French (mostly via Latin) but a surprising number derive from Greek. I have simplified the words a bit (to adapt them to the way they appear in English—for example, k and y become c and u in English, though these letters don't exist in the Greek alphabet. You may sometimes have to add or subtract one or two letters to make an English word. Most of these words can be combined to make a word of two or three syllables, but there are also a few words that can make a single English word.

Several of these words end in os or on—they sometimes keep the 'o' in English, but drop the last letter.

How many English words can you make from these Greek words?

Examples: apathy=not feeling, perimeter=measurement around.

a – not

anthropo – human

archy – rule

anther – flower

anti – against

cata – down

copto – cut

chrys – golden

chrono-time

dia – through

dendro – tree

gram/graph –write

hyper – over

heli – sun

hydro – water

litho – stone

mono – single

matho – skilled in

meter – measure

oligo -few

ornitho -bird

phone - voice

potamos - river

psyche – the soul

pathy -suffering

syn/ sym – with

aner, andro - man

aristo – the best

bio – human life

cracy/crat – rule

demo – the people

geo – earth

hippo – horse

iatry – healing

mega – big

nauto-sailor

philo- love

pathy - feeling

peri – around

aster, astro -star

agora – market

chrono – time

claustro – closed

deino – strange

gene – birth

hemi – half

logy - study

micro – small

nomo, nomy – name

poly – many

phobia – fear

sphere - round

scope – see   sophy- wisdom   strophe -turn

theo – god

  tele – far   zoo– animal life

Trick Question: Why do you think television is half Greek, half Latin, when it would be normal to stick to one language?

CLASSICAL QUERIES

1. When Socrates was asked at his trial what sentence he thought he deserved, what did he suggest?

2. In the time of Caesar and Cicero, what language did the Roman Senators commonly speak?

3. When Croesus, King of Lydia, asked the Oracle whether it was wise to attack the Persian empire, what advice was he given? And what was the outcome?

4. King Alexander's path to Asia was blocked by the Gordian Knot which nobody had been able to untie. How did he solve the problem?

5. When Athens faced the might of the Persian empire, the oracle advised their leader to look to their wooden walls. What walls was the oracle referring to?

6. What did Pheidippides do to originate the Marathon race?

7. What happened to you if you were ostracised in Athens at the time of Pericles?

8. What are the Elgin Marbles—and what's Elgin got to do with them?

9. What did Aphrodite offer Paris, and how did her gift provoke the Trojan War?

10. 'I fear the Greeks even when bearing gifts' What gift was the Trojan priest referring to at the end of the Trojan war?

11. How did Clytemnestra kill her husband, Agamemnon, on his return from Troy—and what had he done to deserve it?

12. In what city was the palace of King Minos?

13. What was Medusa's hairstyle?

14. Why was Prometheus punished by Zeus?

15. What is the modern name for Thera—the Greek Island where a volcanic eruption caused a tsunami around 1600 BC?

WHAT'S IN A NAME?

G   *reek names were supposed to reflect a person's character. As they were selected at birth, this must have reflected the parents' hopes rather than the reality! But in this story, I have the advantage of hindsight—the names are supposed to fit the personalities.*

Cassandra is the main character in the story, and like her legendary namesake, she is sometimes able to foresee the future without being able to change it—though she is not the prophet of doom that her name suggests. Her mother is named Callista which means the most beautiful. The boyfriend's name would send a signal of alarm to a Greek reader because he is called Lycos—which means wolf.

The boy that Cassandra meets on the Acropolis is called Alexis, which means defender—and that is his role in the story. His father is Daedalus—the appropriate name for a craftsman, and his mother is Hestia, which means 'hearth,' and signifies the welcoming, motherly part she plays.

Next, Cassandra faces the two villains—the guards of the palace. Janus literally means guard, and Dracon means dragon or serpent. It is Dracon that leads Cassandra to meet Cecrops, the legendary king of Athens. One of his warriors is called Georgios, a common name for a man who owns a farm.

The girls that Cassandra meets at the palace include Alethea—which means truth, but as her friend points out, she is a very good liar. (Later on, we meet her twin sister, Sophia—called that because she is wise.) Thalia means blossom; in other words, she is optimistic and cheerful. Chloe's name suggests 'green shoots'—like Georgios, she comes from farming stock. Arete—as the name suggests—is the virtuous one that Cassandra can trust. Then there is Irene, the poor girl whose name means peace, which doesn't stop her getting beaten by her teacher.

When she escapes from the palace, Cassandra meets the kind old lady, Agatha—which means good—who introduces her to the giant, Brontës, whose name means thunder. They travel to Aegina, where they meet the potter called Hermes—named after a god who had many roles, but in this story his chief role is to do with trade and hospitality. After Aegina, Cassandra and her friends travel to Delos where they meet Demosthenes, which means 'strength of the people'—he shows this strength by the way he organises his followers. And finally, Cassandra and her friends end up in Amnisos where they are hosted by

Hermes and his wife Aspasia, whose name means welcome, and Cassandra is introduced to Cressida whose name means golden—though she is the first to admit that she is far from being rich.

The legend behind the story of Poseidon's Granddaughter:

Aegeus, a legendary king of Athens, married Aethra—the daughter of Pittheus, king of Troezen, and hoped to have a son by her. But he was tricked by the Gods, and the father of the baby turned out to be Poseidon. The baby's name was Theseus, who later became the legendary, half-immortal king of Athens. Theseus had many affairs with woman—and in the case of Cassandra's mother, I have just added another affair to the list. It might well be asked why Poseidon—having sent an angel to fly Cassandra to Athens—didn't repeat the mission when Cassandra escaped to Amnisos. The answer is to be found in the legend that King Cecrops arranged a competition among the gods as to which god should be the patron god or goddess of Athens. The chief contenders were Poseidon and Athene. When Athene won, Poseidon was understandably miffed and lost interest in transporting his granddaughter to Athens.

Also by the Author

Bewitched by Apollo. Book 2 in 'A Girl's Adventures in Ancient Greece'

The Island Wars (3 Book Volume): 'The House at the Edge of the World', 'The Guardian's Necklace', and 'The Neustrian Princess'

The Author

Atticus Smith with his wife, Joey, and their dog, George, on the island of Jersey.

ACKNOWLEDGMENTS

I would like to thank the multi-talented Lauren Etchells for her delightful cover design, as well as for guiding the work through the publishing process and giving me many thoughtful suggestions along the way. I would also like to thank the Jersey Writers Group for their helpful comments on the work in progress. Finally, I would like to thank my wife, Joey for her continued interest and support.

Printed in Great Britain
by Amazon

21734884R00079